for Andy & Jay

Thundering good wishes.

Janet Hickman

THE THUNDER-PUP

By Janet Hickman

Macmillan Publishing Co., Inc.
New York
Collier Macmillan Publishers
London

FOR HOLLY AND SARA

Macmillan Publishing Co., Inc.
866 Third Avenue, New York, N.Y. 10022
Collier Macmillan Canada, Ltd.
Printed in the United States of America

10 9 8 7 6 5 4 3 2 1

LIBRARY OF CONGRESS CATALOGING IN PUBLICATION DATA
Hickman, Janet. The thunder-pup.
SUMMARY: Linnie eagerly awaits her tenth birthday because she is convinced her family plans to give her a dog, the only thing in the world she wants.
[1. Dogs–Fiction] I. Title.
PZ7.H5314Th [Fic] 81–2614 ISBN 0–02–743770–1 AACR2

Contents

Linnie's Wish 1
One-One Thousand, Two-One Thousand 7
Darla 12
Harry and Bess 19
The Plan 25
The Trouble With Sunday 30
Puppy Business 34
Hide and Seek 39
"Amidst the storm they sang. . . ." 43
Granpop's Discovery 49
Biscuits 54
Ghost Story 59
The Day of the Dogcatcher 64
A Present for Darla 70
Surprise! 75
Welcome Home, Harry 81
A Dog in the House 85
Where, Oh Where . . . ? 90
Unhappy Birthday 97
The Flash and the Roar 104
Many Happy Returns 108

THE THUNDER-PUP

Linnie's Wish

The classroom was hot, with an end-of-the-year smell that came from old chalk, used lunch pails, and summer feet in winter shoes. It was Friday afternoon, past two o'clock. Almost done, thought Linnie, fidgeting over her writing assignment. There were three topics to choose from, lettered in Miss Crane's neat round script near the top of the blackboard.

"My Favorite Person" was the first suggestion. Linnie passed over that one as too hard. She would have to decide among her family—Mom or Dad or Granpop or Aunt Em, or Garrett—and how could she choose one over the other when they were all so important? She couldn't imagine getting along without any of them. Except for Garrett, maybe. Brothers could be done without, sometimes.

"My Favorite Place" was the second topic, one that Linnie rejected as too easy. Her favorite place was home, Granpop's house, right here in Merrittsburg, where she had lived for always. It would sound silly to write about Merrittsburg for Miss Crane. There wasn't much to say about such a small town, population 234. And anyway, Miss Crane already knew all about it.

The third topic was the one that Linnie chose.

MY WISH
by Linnie McKay

What I want most of all is a dog. Dogs are furry and warm and they lick your hand and curl up on your bed if you let them. I have wanted a dog all my life but my Aunt Em says cats in the barn is one thing but a dog in the house is something else and that's why I never had one. Aunt Em is the one who takes care of our house and she thinks dogs are dirty, and also that they smell bad and have germs.

I do not agree. I think dogs are good friends. There are not many people near my house for me to be friends with, not counting Arnold Anderson or the girl who is coming to visit this weekend (Dear Miss Crane, her name is Darla Champion and her mother and father are coming too but she might get to stay for a while). That's why I would like to have a dog someday, to talk to it and play with it and teach it things.

Maybe for my birthday I will get one. Everyone says if things go all right I might get a big surprise for my birthday, and that is not very far away.

Linnie glanced up at the calendar. Right underneath the giant 1950 was the word *MAY* in capital letters, and among the rows of numbers, next Wednesday's date wore a red circle for picnic day, the last of the year. She had a poem to recite for the program. She looked at the next row of numbers and added another circle in her mind, for her birthday. Tomorrow's date should have a circle, too, she thought. It was exciting to have company coming, especially someone she had only heard about but never met.

Then Linnie sat back and chewed her pencil, considering. Should she write more, or was it time for "The End"? The words didn't say what was inside her when she thought about having a dog. Maybe there weren't any words like that. Or maybe it was just too hot to think. She pushed her glasses back up and sighed; they never stayed put when her nose was shiny with heat. She wrote "The End" on her paper with a curlicue under it to show how certain she was.

She was tired of writing. To be truthful, she was tired of fourth grade. Ever since Valentine's Day, when she had finished the last book on the shelf at the back of the room, she had been waiting for next year. Of course she would be with Miss Crane again because Miss Crane taught fifth, too. But at least she would get to sit next to the windows.

Zwish. A paper airplane landed softly in the middle of her writing. She turned and made a face at the pilot, a brown-eyed, big-toothed boy two rows over and three seats back, on the fifth grade side. That Arnold! Probably he was going to fool around and get both of them in trouble with Miss Crane. Aunt Em said that Linnie should just ignore that Anderson boy. He'd never be worth a nickel, Aunt Em said, unless someone wanted to pay him for making noise.

But Linnie had always had Arnold for a friend, because there were no girls her age in Merrittsburg. Clara Johnson was too old and the Simpson twins were too young.

Sally Maloney, who was ten and just right, lived so far out on the road beyond the cemetery that Aunt Em wouldn't let Linnie go there by herself. Everyone else in Miss Crane's room, girls and boys alike, came to school by bus each morning and rode away into the country again every afternoon. For a full-time companion, it was Arnold Anderson or nobody. He was a pest sometimes, when she wanted to read, or just be by herself; but mostly Linnie thought he was all right.

Besides, Arnold had two puppies. Linnie had only seen them once, but she had heard everything there was to know about them. Arnold had found them in a ditch while he was delivering his papers—little brown pups with snub noses and loppy ears, one male and one female. Harry and Bess was what he had named them, after President Truman and his wife. Linnie thought it was disrespectful to name a puppy after the President of the United States. She wanted Arnold to call them Waif and Wafer, because they were homeless and cookie-colored, or Brier and Bramble, because they had sharp, stickery teeth, or even Hansel and Gretel, because they had been abandoned. But Arnold just said that Linnie read too many books and went on calling them Harry and Bess.

"Arnold Anderson—" Miss Crane pronounced the name and let it hang in the air. Linnie looked at the floor. She always pretended to be invisible when Miss Crane talked to Arnold.

"I don't know what you've been doing, Arnold," the teacher said, "but it wasn't your writing assignment. So you will get plenty of time to finish it after school." Someone snickered, and Miss Crane turned to the sound.

Linnie glanced quickly at the paper airplane before she crumpled it. I JUST REMBEBERED I GOT TO TELL YOU SOMTHING, was the message on one wing. On the other wing was a single word: AWEFULL. It was awful all right, thought Linnie. Arnold was going to get an F in spelling for sure. Still, she couldn't help smiling. One of the things about Arnold was that he exaggerated a lot. Once he had passed her a note about his broken fingernail that began, I AM IN GRATE PANE. Whatever awful story he had this time would just have to wait, now that he was staying after school.

Linnie was even pleased, in a way, to be able to walk home alone without anyone to interrupt the story she was going to tell herself about tomorrow and the friend who might get to stay as long as her birthday. Then when she got her own dog they could both act surprised, as if Linnie had never guessed why everyone at home kept swallowing secrets and being quiet when she was around. She had heard enough whispers: "finally," ". . . will love it," "crowded, but. . . ." The best clue, Linnie thought, was that Aunt Em had been in a grump for weeks; probably she was worried about learning to put up with a dog after all her years of chasing them out of the yard.

Here it is, Rosebud, her dad would say, using her baby name and smiling the way his old pictures looked, the ones taken before he got hurt in the war. Her cheeks might even grow bright spots of pink the way they always did just when she didn't want them to. *All yours, Linnie,* her mom would say. *We knew just what you wanted this year. . . .*

Linnie peeked up at the clock, even though Miss Crane

had already told the class twice in the last half hour that clock watchers would Never Get Anywhere in Life. Linnie didn't want to get anywhere in life. She just wanted to get to tomorrow, and her company, and then to her birthday, and the dog-to-be.

One-One Thousand, Two-One Thousand

First there was lightning, a sudden glare in the gray morning. Half asleep, Linnie flopped over on her stomach. Then came the thunder, an evil boom of it that echoed high over the maple trees. She was wide awake and stiff as a stick in the same instant. She could feel her heart bouncing inside her chest and a whimper coming up in her throat. I won't cry, she promised herself. I'm too old to cry.

Crack! The sky shuddered and lit itself again.

"One-one thousand," counted Linnie under her breath. "Two-one thousand, three-one thousand." Garrett had told her about the counting. The longer it took to count between the lightning and the thunder, he said, the safer you were, because light traveled faster than sound. Garrett knew about things like that. If it took a long time for the sound of the thunder to reach you, then the lightning was far away and you shouldn't worry about it. Linnie had asked what would happen if the lightning and thunder were right together, and Garrett said not to worry about that, either. If the lightning and thunder were absolutely, exactly, perfectly together, he said, you wouldn't have time to worry about it, because it would be pow! good-by!

Thunder again, a deep rattle of it, a voice without words that told stories of nameless, fearsome things. Linnie burrowed her head between the pillow and the mattress to shut out the sound, not caring how Garrett would laugh if he could see her. Once he had called her a stupid ostrich for hiding her face, but Mom had said just because he was almost through high school he didn't need to forget there was a time he had been afraid of a few things himself.

In spite of the pillow, she could hear rain splattering against the window by her bed. Probably it was spraying in through the narrow open space at the bottom. She knew she ought to shut the window; the wallpaper under the sill would get wet and then there would be a splotch for Aunt Em to fuss about. But she couldn't make herself sit up and reach out toward the storm, not even that little bit.

Linnie bit her lip and scolded herself. She wished she could be like Dad and Granpop. They enjoyed storms. Right now they might be sitting out on the front porch, watching the trees bend and the rain dance on the road, with Granpop giving comments on the lightning. "That's a sizzler!" he might say. "Did you see that one, Andy?" Or, "Three prongs! Sonofagun! Three prongs! Ain't that a sight?"

Granpop always said that lightning greened up the grass and put a sharp smell in the air. Aunt Em said there was no such thing as a sharp smell, and she didn't like for them to sit outside in heavy weather. "Leo," Aunt Em would say to Granpop, "you are an old fool right and proper. You come in off that porch this minute, before you're struck down! And you, Andy," she would say to Linnie's father, "you ought to have better sense than to sit on that metal chair. Imagine you going to war and getting through that by the skin of your teeth and then come home and just ask for it on your own front porch. Why, I knew a woman once who just happened to be by a metal frame on a door—that Jarvis woman, Leo, you remember when it was?—and the lightning took her quick as a bullet. . . ."

Aunt Em knew a lot of lightning stories, all of them bad. Linnie didn't want to think about them, but they came to her mind uninvited. Even though Aunt Em had told her there was not much harm in a storm if you stayed inside and used your good sense, Linnie found it hard to remember that part.

And then Aunt Em was calling her. "Linnie! Get up now!" The familiar voice came up the stairs the way it did every morning at breakfast time. Aunt Em had her own little house, just across the street from Granpop's orchard, but she was hardly ever in it except while she slept. Most of the time she spent cooking and cleaning and looking after things at Granpop's house so that Mom could help Dad in his shop in Springtown.

"I don't want to get up!" wailed Linnie. "It's storming!"

"My land, child," Aunt Em called back, "uncover your head! It's all over but for a few sprinkles." Linnie pushed her pillow away and extended her neck, cautious as a turtle.

"You've got things to do today, don't forget!" Aunt Em went on from the foot of the stairs. "That bed needs making before company comes, and there's a thing or two you could do to straighten your room a bit, not to mention you could dust in the dining room for me, and—"

"OH!" Linnie sat up. The sky was quiet. All that was left of the rain was an occasional soft plunk from the leaky gutter outside her window. It was over. She was safe. And company was coming. "Okay!" she called. "I'm up."

She bounced out of bed and into yesterday's clothes, all the while surveying her room. She didn't see how she could get anything else put away. Already every drawer and shelf were packed tight as a suitcase and spilling over, with all her real treasures out in plain sight. Linnie said good morning with her eyes to the best things: her stuffed dolls, especially good, reliable Flat Mabel; the eleven china cats Mrs. Tanner had given her; Garrett's hand-me-down rock collection; magazine pictures of dogs, every kind; and most of all, books. Attic books, library books, Christmas-present books and birthday books, plus others whose origins were beyond remembering.

Linnie loved her room; it was perfect, just right, comfortable as a nest, even if it wasn't very big. She put on her glasses and took another look. Sometimes it was hard to imagine how she had once shared this room with Garrett, when she was still small enough to sleep in a crib. Now Garrett slept downstairs, in Granpop's room, with his clothes in a chest in the pantry and all his experiments and old batteries and things in a corner of the cellar between the furnace and the canned string beans. Mom said it was a disgrace, how cramped they all were, but Linnie didn't care. Her bed was a double, so there would be plenty of room for another girl.

She rummaged for the hairbrush and pulled it twice

through her long, unruly curls. It was not enough to get out all the tangles, but it was enough to get by. The storm was over, and she was in a hurry. She rushed downstairs to get started on the day.

Darla

The kitchen was a confusion of pots and pans and talk. Everyone was there except for Dad, who had gone early to the shop so that he could have the afternoon off, for company.

"Andy just can't wait to see Bud Champion again," Linnie's mother said to no one in particular, spreading chocolate icing on a three-layer cake. Then she said "Ouch!" and "Honestly, this kitchen!" because she banged her elbow on the edge of the cupboard while she was trying to keep out of Aunt Em's way. She rubbed her elbow and stood back to look at the cake. "I'll bet Marianna is just as thin and pretty as she was five years ago," she said.

"Hmp!" said Aunt Em, who didn't sound very much interested in the way Mrs. Champion looked. "Who wants more eggs?" Garrett voted yes and Granpop voted no. Linnie hoped that Aunt Em wouldn't scold because she was eating shredded wheat instead. Aunt Em didn't believe in eating breakfast out of a box.

"I wish I knew what Darla looked like," Linnie said. Dad was a friend of Mr. Champion's because they had been in the Army together. Mom knew Mrs. Champion because the two men had been in an Army hospital at the same time, and the wives had done a lot of waiting side by side. But to Linnie, "the Champions" was just a signature on a Christmas card that came from Pittsburgh, Pennsylvania.

Mom made a final swirl on top of the cake. "Darla is taller than you, I suppose, and darker," she said. "But I've never seen her except in pictures, and nothing recent at that. She's a year older than you, plus a couple of months. I remember when I was away for all that time so I could be with your dad, Marianna used to show me her snapshots of Darla all the time."

Linnie nodded. "But she was only five or six then."

Mom shook her head, remembering. "I used to sit right there and cry, I missed you so."

Linnie smiled. Hearing that part of the story always made her feel good. "Do you really think Darla can stay for a while?"

"I hope so," Mom said, raising her voice over the rattle of dishes that Aunt Em was stacking. "It will be good for you to have somebody to do things with for once, and maybe it will help them out, too, while they get settled and find a place to live and everything. With just the two of them, they might be able to rent a little room somewhere and take their time looking."

Linnie knew that the Champions were moving to Indianapolis so that Mr. Champion could start a new job, and that Darla couldn't stay for a visit unless they decided it was all right for her to finish the trip to Indiana on a bus. Linnie considered what it would be like to ride all that way alone, with only strangers for company. Maybe Darla herself would say no to the idea. She thought so long about it that her cereal went to mush, and even though she pushed it across the table toward Garrett, who would eat anything, she couldn't get rid of it.

Garrett just waved the bowl away and announced that he was going down to his workshop. Linnie suspected that he was trying to build a television set down there. She had seen a kit of tubes and wires and odd-looking papers with fine-print instructions and diagrams full of squiggles. But Garrett wouldn't say what it was supposed to be when it was finished. For one thing, Aunt Em didn't approve of television. "It won't last," she always said. "You mark my word, it's nothing but a novelty. Ruins your eyes with that awful blue light and ruins the looks of a house with that ugly antenna-thing up on the roof." The McKays didn't have a television, although some families in Merrittsburg did. Linnie's dad had already fixed several of them in his repair shop, though, and he had taken her there to watch Milton Berle and some plays and another show with a lot of singing. She hoped that was what Garrett was building, but she didn't know if he could do it. It was true that he had been working on broken radios in Dad's shop for more than a year—last summer and almost every Saturday, and even some days after school if he could get a ride to town. Dad had taught him a lot of things, but maybe not quite enough for his own television set.

"Mind you, now," Aunt Em said to Garrett, "you come up here looking decent at lunchtime. Don't be grease up to your elbows and don't be trackin' up coal dust."

Mom's face clouded. "Go on," she said to Garrett, and then, "There's no need to be after him, Em. He hasn't–"

"Come on along, girl," Granpop said to Linnie, scraping back his chair. "I see you got a bowl of cat food there, so you might as well bring it along out to the barn." He got up slowly. Where Aunt Em was brisk and thin as a string, always moving, Granpop was gentler and more solid, never in a hurry. It was hard for Linnie to remember sometimes that the two of them were brother and sister.

She was glad enough to go with Granpop now, to get out of the kitchen, out of sight. Maybe Aunt Em would forget that she was supposed to dust the dining room, with its hateful knobby-legged furniture. Hooray, she thought. Free. She jounced across the back lot toward the old gray barn, unused now except as a home for cats. They were wild and quick as shadows in the wind, no matter how much Linnie tried to cuddle them. *Not like a dog:* The thought popped into her mind without warning and made her smile.

Linnie scraped her breakfast into the cats' pan. "Granpop," she said, as he appeared in the doorway, "when I–I mean, if I ever do get a dog, I couldn't keep it here, could I? Because of the cats. Maybe in the woodshed?"

Granpop put his hand above his ear and scratched with one thick finger. "Whatever put that in your head?" he asked. His eyes were on the four cats who came slinking out of the old hay and around stacks of scrap lumber. Linnie watched them, too; it seemed easier than looking at Granpop.

"Well," she said, "everyone says there's going to be a surprise for my birthday."

He didn't say anything. She looked up quickly and caught him frowning. And then she thought how silly it was for her to talk about something that was supposed to be a surprise, because Granpop wouldn't want to ruin it. Now he wouldn't know what to say; that's why he was being quiet.

She reached down to stroke the old black tomcat, the tamest of the lot, and changed the subject. "What time are the Champions going to get here? They're going to meet Dad in Springtown first, aren't they? I can't wait to see her. Darla, I mean." She let the words pour out thick enough to cover what she had said before.

"Tell you what," Granpop said. "I need some help out in the front yard by the orchard. There was a little twist of wind, seems like, took a limb out of one of the maples and left twigs and leaves all over. Sure would like to get it cleaned up before company comes."

The sky cleared and the day turned bright as diamonds. Linnie thought that picking up twigs was almost as bad as dusting knobby-legged furniture, but at least it gave her a chance for sunshine. And it was good to be busy because it was true that she couldn't keep her mind off Darla Champion. When would she get there? What was she like? What should they talk about first?

"What time is it now, Granpop?" She asked so often that he finally told her not to ask again; he had taken his pocket watch out of his overalls for the very last time. "They'll get here when they get here," he said.

And finally it was Linnie who saw them coming. Dad was leading the way in his worn-out black Chevy that went *chug-a-putt, chug-a-putt* like something in a cartoon. He grinned and waved when he turned into the driveway, with a blue station wagon following behind.

"They're here!" Linnie squealed, and then her voice quit working. Her mouth went dry and her knees went squirmy. She had a sudden urge to run to the kitchen and hide behind the dining room door, the way she used to do when she was little.

Mom came running out of the house and there was laughing and hugging and backslapping and everyone talking at once. "Marianna! Look at you! I knew you'd look wonderful," Mom said to Mrs. Champion, who was tall and thin and decorated with silver bangle bracelets and dangly earrings.

Mr. Champion had a light-bulb smile. He shook hands all around, and clasped Garrett on both shoulders when he said hello.

Aunt Em came across the yard with her hand extended. "I'm Emma McKay, sister to Leo here," she said, "and the only mother Andy can remember. Any friends of his are more than welcome here."

Linnie hung back. The Champions' daughter was slow about getting out of the back seat. She stretched and blinked as if she had been asleep. Linnie stared before the other pair of eyes had a chance to focus. The girl's hair was smooth and dark as the wing on a crow, held back from her forehead with a twisted scarf that matched her red slacks. She looked like an advertisement in *American Girl* magazine.

Linnie opened her mouth in greeting, but no sound came. How was a person supposed to talk to a magazine picture?

"I'm Darla Gayle Champion," the girl said to Linnie. "G-a-y-l-e, Gayle. I'm eleven." She tilted her head up, just the smallest bit. "You're almost ten, aren't you?"

Linnie nodded and said something polite, but she felt the coming of a worry. It was a sudden and unwelcome feeling, something like the prick of a pin. What if she didn't want Darla Gayle Champion to stay after all?

Harry and Bess

The Champions' visit was a huge success. Long after the cake and pineapple salad were gone, Linnie's dad and his old friend told Army stories. Some of the things they said made everyone laugh; some were funny just to the two of them; some of their stories were sad. Garrett sat bug-eyed and never said a word. He was always trying to get Dad to talk about the time when he was almost captured, but Dad had never seemed to feel much like it before.

Aunt Em kept passing the coffee and warning Mrs. Champion to sit still and not trouble herself helping to clear the table. Finally Mr. Champion looked at his watch and announced that he had drunk so much coffee he would just float on to Indiana if he didn't have such a stomachful of fried chicken to anchor him down. And then Mrs. Champion laughed and said they really did have to go because they had promised to visit one of her cousins along the way, and look what time it was already, and so on. Mrs. Champion was quite a talker, Linnie decided, and beautiful, too. She had a wide, curvy mouth bright with plum-colored lipstick. Aunt Em would have a fit, Linnie thought, if Mom wore lipstick like that.

"Surely you aren't going so soon!" Mom protested.

"Sorry to eat and run," Darla's father said, hunching his shoulders and turning up both palms. "But things just move too fast."

Linnie looked across the dining room table at Darla, who was nibbling on the very last of her cake. It had taken her twenty minutes to eat one baby-sized slice. She hadn't said anything other than "Yes, thank you," "No, thank you," and "This is delicious" all through the meal.

"Is Darla going to stay?" she asked, right out in the middle of everything.

"Mind your manners," said Aunt Em. "It's not nice to interrupt."

"But it's a good question," Dad said, "and the answer's yes. All settled." He looked proud as a magician pulling a rabbit out of a hat. "We talked about it in town," he went on, looking from Darla to Linnie and back again. "They'll call when they've found a house and we'll make final arrangements then for putting Darla on the bus." He turned toward Darla's father. "I wish we had the time and the money to bring her out ourselves, Bud. Maybe some other year—but you know what we're getting into. . . ."

Mr. Champion came over to Dad and put one arm on the back of his chair. "Listen," he said, "listen—" But Linnie didn't hear what Dad was supposed to listen to because the two of them went out on the porch by themselves.

Darla put down her fork and smiled at Linnie. "I thought it would be fun to have a vacation in the country," she said.

The country! Linnie thought. Imagine! "We don't even keep chickens any more," she said, but no one seemed to hear.

Darla's mother was kissing her good-by, and Darla's father was back inside kissing everybody good-by, even Linnie.

"Have yourselves a good time, you two girls," he said.

Everyone went out on the porch to watch the Champions' car back out of the drive and head south toward the highway, tooting once. Linnie thought about how she would feel if Mom and Dad were in that car, driving away, leaving her with people she had just seen for the first time in her life. I'd cry, Linnie thought, watching Darla be cheerful.

"Well," said Linnie's mother, as if she could read minds, "this is a good time for you to be busy getting acquainted, Darla. Why don't you have Linnie take you around our little town here and show you where everything is?"

"Sure," said Linnie, glad for a suggestion. "Come on." She started across the now-empty road. Darla glanced once in the direction her parents had gone, smoothed back her hair, and followed Linnie.

"Over there is the little house where Jack Tramp used to live," Linnie said, pointing. "And he lived in that old garage behind it once, too. Garrett told me."

Darla stared politely. "Doesn't he ever cut his grass?"

"Oh," said Linnie, "Jack Tramp's been dead for a long time. Ever since I was in second grade. No one knows if he had any relatives so the county owns his property, and they never get the weeds cut. Not very often, anyway.

Aunt Em says it's shameful." She turned and swept her arm in a half circle. "See over there behind Granpop's barn? There's a creek beyond those trees, and down that way there's the Stones—it's a really big stack of rocks that was supposed to be one end of a bridge once, a long time ago. Want to see it?"

"No, thank you," Darla said. "There are plenty of rocks in Pennsylvania."

"Oh." Linnie took a breath. "Well, come this way, then," she said, starting along the edge of the road. "Up beyond the garden here, that's Aunt Em's house—the one across from the orchard. The next one there is Mrs. Tanner's. And if you look hard you can see the corner of Fiddler's Auto Garage."

They walked in silence for a while. Darla didn't spend much time looking at the sights. "I don't think I've ever been in a town that didn't have sidewalks," she said.

"We've got sidewalks," Linnie told her. "Up around the corner by the grocery and down by the post office, and in front of the school. You'll see," she said.

Darla followed along, smiling. "There are sidewalks *everywhere* in Pittsburgh," she said.

Linnie dropped her eyes. Darla's smile made her uneasy, the way she felt when she watched a thunderhead rosy and glowing in the sunset, wondering if the storm would come or go.

Then they came to the corner and turned it, and Linnie's spirits rose. There was Arnold Anderson in his front yard with a puppy under each arm. "Arnold!" she called, waving, and began to run. Darla poked along behind, and stopped to look in the grocery-store window.

"Hi," Arnold said glumly. "You know what, Linnie? My

father's a murderer, that's what. He wants to call the dog-catcher for Harry and Bess. Just because they made a mess on the floor and he wasn't looking where he stepped. I don't see how that makes it all their fault. And then my mother goes and says she doesn't want two dogs anyway, so that's that. Say good-by, Harry." He handed one of the wriggling bundles to Linnie.

Harry the pup settled his little body against her chest and began to lick her neck, *slup-lup, slup-lup,* like a moth fluttering. "Aw, Arnold," she breathed. "This little fellow can't live in a cage at the pound. It wouldn't be right."

"Huh," said Arnold, fondling the other pup's loppy brown ears. "It's worse than that. You know what happens when nobody comes to the pound to get a dog? You know what happens to the dog? Pffft!"

Linnie refused to think about it. "You ought to find a home for them yourself, then, before the dogcatcher can get them. You could be sure that way."

"I've been trying," he said, "but everyone who wants dogs already has dogs. Unless *you* want them." Arnold's eyes lit with the idea. "You want them, Linnie?"

She wanted them, all right. She didn't ever want to put down the one that she was holding. *Keep me,* his snuggle said, as plain as words. But she had to say no. She was getting a dog of her own for her birthday, wasn't she? This would spoil the surprise. And Aunt Em would certainly never get used to the idea of *two* dogs.

"I can't, Arnold," she said. "They wouldn't let me."

"Bananas!" he said. "Why not?"

Linnie was trying to explain, with her fingers tracing the shape of the pup's head over and over, when Darla caught up and had to be introduced.

Arnold held out the female pup in greeting. "Want to hold Bess?"

"No, thanks." Darla shook her head. "Are they both yours?"

"Right now they are. I found 'em but I can't keep them."

Darla fussed with her blouse collar and moved backward a half step or so. "They've probably got fleas," she said. "Strays almost always do. Or sore eyes or some disease. I'm very sensitive to things like that."

Fleas! Linnie hadn't considered that, and now the very thought of itching made her itch. "They look perfectly all right to me," she said, glaring at Darla.

Darla looked away. "Why don't we go back to your house?" she suggested. "I'm tired from my long trip and everything."

Right now? thought Linnie, dismayed. Right now when she could be holding this puppy and loving it and having a wonderful time? But after all of Mom's and Aunt Em's lectures about good manners, she knew that it wouldn't be kind to complain.

"Okay," she said. "If you really want to." She gave Harry back into Arnold Anderson's keeping and said "See you later" to both of them.

Always be considerate of your guest, Aunt Em had said. *Let the other person choose what to do, especially at first,* Mom had said. But good manners shouldn't tell a person what to think, Linnie decided. And what she was thinking as she walked home with Darla was all about Arnold and the puppies and how awful it would be if the dogcatcher got them.

The Plan

That night was Darla night. At the supper table Darla answered questions about her school and her old neighborhood. Afterward she unpacked her tap shoes and showed them how well she had been doing with her dancing lessons, although she said it ruined the effect when you didn't wear your costume. Linnie had taken a peek at the costume, folded in one corner of the suitcase. It was a miracle of red and white sequins, with a ruffle where the skirt should have been. What would Aunt Em think? Then Darla produced her baton and demonstrated the twirling routine that went with the dance. One hand, two hands, around the neck, be careful of the lamp. Everyone clapped.

Finally Mom said that it was bedtime. "We have to pinch some for space," she said to Darla, patting her on the shoulder, "but you make yourself right at home." Then she gave Linnie a little squeeze that meant "see to it," and sent them upstairs.

Darla bounced experimentally on Linnie's bed. "This room is small, isn't it?" she said.

Linnie frowned. "It seems big enough to me."

"Umm." Darla looked at everything. Suddenly she poked at the rag doll sitting on Linnie's pillow. "What's this?"

"That's Flat Mabel," Linnie said. "I've had her since I was little."

Darla's eyebrow went up. "Flat?!" She looked under the doll's calico apron. " 'Squashed' would be more like it."

Linnie's chin went into its stubborn position. "Her name used to be Stuffed Mabel, when she was new, but then she got lost once when the creek flooded and it spoiled her stuffing to be wet for so long. She got new clothes afterward, but she's still flat."

Darla wrinkled her nose. "You don't sleep with it, do you?"

Linnie crossed her fingers behind her back. "Of course not," she said. "She just sits on my bed during the daytime." She snatched Flat Mabel up from the bed and held her.

"I gave up all my stuffed toys years ago," Darla said. "They're all packed away now. It makes my room so much neater." She glanced at Linnie's shelves and then at the floor, as if Linnie's shelves embarrassed her. "I never saw a bedroom with so many books in it," she went on quickly. "It will take a long time to read them all, won't it?"

"Oh, I've already read them all." Linnie felt a bit hopeful. Maybe Darla Gayle Champion liked to read, and they could talk about their favorites and Mom would take them to the library in Springtown. "Most of them I've read twice, at least. Sometimes I just get the feeling that I want to read—you know?—and then I read all the time, sort of."

Darla raised both eyebrows. "Isn't that dull?" she asked. "Sort of?"

Linnie didn't know what to say. If it were dull she wouldn't be doing it, would she?

"Good night, girls." That was Dad, from outside the door. "Quiet down now and get yourselves into bed."

Darla's pajamas had short legs and ruffles and a pattern of red flowers. She folded every piece of clothing she took off as if she planned to put it on exhibit somewhere. Linnie climbed into Garrett's old pajamas and tried to fold her clothes, too, as if it were her habit, but the jeans kept sliding and slipping until they looked piled as usual.

Finally she snapped off the light and climbed into her bed, beside Darla. "Do you suppose Arnold found somebody to take his puppies?" she whispered.

Darla turned over. "How would I know?" she whispered. "Anyway, your father said we should be quiet."

"Good night," Linnie said grimly, and stuck out her tongue in the darkness.

She dreamed of dogs.

She wasn't accustomed to sharing her bed, and she kept waking from the touch of an elbow or a knee, half remembering that it was Darla, half dreaming still: She had her own dog, curled on the bed beside her. Someone was coming to take it away. "No," she said aloud, without meaning to.

She woke, trembling a little, and thought about the puppies. Surely someone wanted them. They absolutely, certainly could not go to the dog pound. She would do something about it herself if she had to. Soft-hearted. That's what Aunt Em said she was. "You're just like your mother," Aunt Em had scolded once when Linnie wanted to take care of a robin that left its nest too soon. "Wasting sympathy. You can't fix everything, you know." One of the barn cats had found the bird then and taken care of it in his own way.

Linnie's head got clearer and she thought some more. By the time the sky showed itself as gray squares at the window, she knew that she must talk to Arnold first thing. She eased out of bed, hoping not to wake Darla, grabbed her glasses, and got dressed without a sound. She tiptoed past her parents' room and then downstairs; not even Granpop was stirring, and he was always first in the kitchen.

The front door squeaked a little when she unlatched it, but she saw with relief that the paper wasn't there yet. It was on its way, though; she had a glimpse of Arnold far up the street, not hurrying, zigzagging from one side of the pavement to the other. First a house on this side, now a house on that side. It seemed forever before he got to the McKays' porch.

"Ssst!" she warned before he could say anything. "Whisper. Did you find anyone to take Harry and Bess?"

Arnold shook his head. "It's curtains for them, I guess. My father already called the dogcatcher and he's coming first thing tomorrow morning. He says that when I grow up I'll understand that it's a kindness, or something like that."

Linnie scowled. "When I grow up, I won't understand," she said. "Listen, Arnold, I've been thinking. Maybe we could hide them and take care of them, sort of, to give you more time to find someone who wants them."

"Sure. Where am I going to hide two dogs with the dogcatcher looking for them?"

"I know a place," Linnie said. "I think."

"Yeah. I get it! Your barn."

"No, you simple. There's cats out there. Put them in Jack Tramp's old garage. The lock doesn't work on that little door, so you could get in, and it's far enough from anyone else's house that they could whine and no one would hear them. And besides, I could feed them for you and stuff like that." It would be good practice, she told herself, for taking care of her own dog. She had a sudden warm memory of Harry's brown and white body and his snoozling black nose and his damp velvet tongue. "Come on, Arnold. Wouldn't that be all right?"

Arnold studied the garage across the road, or what he could see of it through the weeds and grass. "You're a life-saver, Linnie," he said finally. "You know that? You ought to get a medal from the national dog society or something. It's A-Number-One-Perfect. Except I don't know how to get them over there without anybody knowing about it."

"Shh," Linnie reminded. "Everybody's going to know about it if you don't shush. Tomorrow morning when you deliver your papers—that'll be before the dogcatcher, won't it?—you just put Harry and Bess in the bag, too. There won't be anybody up to see you, will there? And then leave the dogs in the garage on your way from our house over to Mr. Murdoch's."

"Yeah," said Arnold, nodding. "That'll work. My father's gonna yell, though. He'll want to know what happened to 'em."

Linnie chewed on her lip; she hadn't thought of that. "Just say they got away," she suggested. "That's the important thing."

"Linnie? Is that you?" called someone from the kitchen.

"Go on, Arnold," she whispered, and then raised her voice. "It's me, Granpop. I was just getting the paper."

The Trouble With Sunday

Sunday was a long, long day. What Linnie wanted to do was read, to stretch out in the glider on the front porch and go through one whole book and two jelly sandwiches without stopping. What Darla wanted to do was show Linnie all her baton tricks out in the side yard. After that, she coaxed Linnie to try.

"See? Like this! No! The other way!" Linnie was all thumbs and Darla was all giggles. "Let's turn cartwheels, then. Bet I can get clear to the trees over there without stopping. I'll race you—"

"I'll watch," Linnie said, plopping down on the grass. Darla could stretch and snap her body like a rubber band. Linnie couldn't. She hadn't turned a cartwheel or a somersault for ever so long; she wobbled when she went up and went every-which-way coming down. Once someone at school had laughed and called her "Leadbottom" and she hadn't tried again. Besides, her glasses might fall off.

Darla Gayle Champion made cartwheels look as easy as walking. Garrett came out to watch. She finished her cartwheels and switched to backbends and then two other things that made her look like a pretzel.

"Hey," Garrett said, "that's good. You must have rubber bones."

Darla flashed a wide smile in Garrett's direction. "Oh no, I'm not even double-jointed. I just practice a lot."

Linnie yawned. "Why don't we go over and see Mrs. Tanner?" she suggested. "She'll show you her china cats." Mrs. Tanner was an interesting person to talk to, Linnie thought. But Darla couldn't take her baton; she might break something with it in Mrs. Tanner's tucked-up house.

Darla squeezed out another smile for Linnie. "Why don't I teach Garrett to do this?" The baton flashed.

Garrett took a turn and couldn't do it. He gave up, laughing. "Give me another lesson sometime," he said, and went back to the house.

Darla did some more cartwheels, looking happier than Linnie felt. Who wants to twirl batons and do cartwheels, anyway? she grumped to herself, and wondered if Darla would play Old Maid. She had a new deck, and they could play on the well curb out of the sun.

But then Mom came out to announce that they were all taking a drive to Springtown. Linnie didn't want to go. Even in Granpop's Ford they would be crowded; she and Darla would have to sit close as Siamese twins.

"I'll stay here," she volunteered as the others piled into the car. "That way the back seat won't be so hot."

"Get in," Dad said, with half a smile. "We'll stop at the Creamery, coming home. You wouldn't pass up a chance for an orange-pineapple cone, would you?"

"Is that why we're going?"

"No and yes." The other corner of his mouth twitched. "There are some things your granpop wants to look at.

And Darla didn't get to see all the sights the other day."

Whatever, Linnie thought, it was a wasted trip. Granpop drove and took his time, edging along through Merrittsburg so that he could wave at Mr. Darcy, the postmaster, and at Arnold's father, and at the little Simpson girls, who jumped up and down and squealed, "Huhwo! Huhwo, Mister Kay!" He crept on like a snail over the highway to Springtown, admiring gardens as he went. Then he drove up and down and around one block after another. Finally he doubled back and went around the same block three times.

Mom and Dad sat up front talking about boring things like yards and gardens and downspouts and how much it would cost to put a new roof on one of the big old-fashioned houses they were passing. Garrett whistled to himself by one window in the back, with Darla leaning across him to look out and ask questions: "Is that a dance studio? Honest? Where's the movie theater? Springtown *has* to have a movie theater! Have you ever been in that coffee shop? Is it nice? Ooh! A candy store! I love chocolate candy. It's my weakness."

Linnie cleared her throat. "There's the library," she said, but Darla was looking the other way.

Aunt Em sat very straight and quiet by the other window in the back, with her mouth pinched up. Linnie supposed that Aunt Em didn't care to ride around like a sardine in a can any more than she did. She took Aunt Em's hand and squeezed it.

Just then Granpop steered the car to the curb and let the engine idle while he and Dad looked and pointed and looked again at an old house with fancy wood trimming on the porch and along the eaves.

"Whose house is this, Mr. McKay?" asked Darla, craning her neck.

Dad turned his head a little. "You like it? One of my customers owns it."

"It's beautiful," Darla said. "It's elegant, like something in a movie."

Linnie thought it was ugly. And besides, it was sandwiched between two other tall old houses, almost as close as riders crowded in a back seat.

Mom scooted herself around to face the back. "Did you ever see anything like that porch? Isn't it something? What do you think, Em?"

Aunt Em rubbed her nose with one knuckle. "Doesn't matter what I think, I guess," she said shortly.

Dad cleared his throat. "Well," he said, "we'd better go, Pop, before the Creamery closes."

The ice cream was the only good thing about the whole trip, in Linnie's opinion. She had two scoops on a sugar cone, fudge on the bottom and orange-pineapple on top. Garrett said that was a disgusting combination and it was no wonder she was such a chub-tub. Darla said he wasn't nice to say that, but she giggled, anyway. And then she ordered a single scoop of orange ice, small.

"Dancers have to be very careful about their eating habits," Darla said.

Linnie licked her ice cream in silence and hoped that Mr. and Mrs. Champion would be settled in Indianapolis very soon.

Puppy Business

On Monday morning Arnold was late to school. Linnie missed two problems on her end-of-the-year arithmetic test just worrying about him. Maybe the dogcatcher had come too early, before Arnold had a chance to start out with his papers. Maybe those two puppies were on their way to a cage right this very minute. Maybe this, maybe that. It was recess time before she knew for sure. Arnold came running onto the playground making his antiaircraft noises, and that meant he was feeling good. Linnie told Sally Maloney to find someone else to teeter-totter with, and ran to meet him before Jake Schultz and the other fifth-grade boys could claim him to play second base.

"It was a close call," Arnold said, trying to smooth his uncombed hair. "My father's real suspicious. I come back from my route this morning, see, and there's the dogcatcher already and my father's just standing there tapping his finger, waitin' for me. I don't think he believed it when I said they just got out, as far as I knew. Anyway, he told the dogcatcher to keep checkin' around if it wouldn't be too much trouble and that old stinker said sure, it wasn't any trouble to him." Arnold stopped to grin. "But he's not gonna find 'em cause they're shut in that garage, all right. I went back to make sure."

Linnie grinned, too. "Did you leave them anything to eat?"

"Sure. I gave them nearly all my peanut butter and pickle sandwich that I was having for breakfast."

"Aagh!" Linnie stuck her tongue out all the way. "What are you trying to do? Poison them? I bet they won't eat it."

"Peanut butter and pickle is good," Arnold said, getting ready to argue. "I like it."

"Never mind, Arnold. Maybe they'll eat the bread. What about water?"

"They don't really have enough, I guess." He began to look worried, remembering. "Just a little bit that I got in an old coffee cup I found in there and took out to the puddle in the lane. They'll need water as soon after school as you can get it."

"Aren't you coming to help?"

"Can't." Arnold shook his head. "My father said he wanted me to cut the grass after school and he wasn't in any mood to have me disappear." Arnold turned himself upside down from the monkey bars and swung by his knees. "And keep the door shut, too, or they might really get away and the dogcatcher will find them," he said. "Get that whatchamacallit girl to help you."

"Darla?" Linnie made a face. "I don't think so," she said. "Remember about the fleas and everything? She'd probably tell."

Arnold pulled himself right side up and looked around the playground. "Where is she, anyway?"

"She stayed home. To help Aunt Em or something."

Thank goodness, Linnie added to herself. It was bad enough that Darla was coming to school for the picnic and program on Wednesday. Mom had talked to Miss Crane on the telephone and Darla was even going to have a part in the program. Showing off, Linnie thought to herself, and tried to unthink it. It wasn't polite to criticize a new person without very good reason; Mom and Aunt Em agreed about that. Linnie sighed and set her mind to waiting for afternoon. Harry and Bess were depending on her. How could she slip away to take care of them without anyone noticing?

When the time came, it was easy. She went home from school with her arms loaded, carrying all that she had cleaned out of her desk because the next day was teachers' day, no school. Mom was in the kitchen making peanut clusters, one of her specialties, for the picnic. Darla was busy watching her.

"You look hot," Mom said to Linnie. "How about a glass of milk?" Aunt Em wasn't there; she was fussing with the flower boxes on her own porch. So Linnie was brave and asked for cereal instead. She put it in the oldest bowl she could find, with plenty of milk. Then she got a glass of water and went outside to eat on the well curb, saying the kitchen was too steamy. In another minute she was across the road, up the lane, through the tall grass, and pulling open the narrow door of Jack Tramp's old garage.

The inside was dim and cool, cluttered around the edges. There were cobwebs at the windows. It smelled of old things: dusty paint cans, sacks of newspaper, rotting wood. And now, puppies.

The two of them came up over the edge of a cardboard box, knocking it down and spilling out its newspaper lining, well chewed. They cried at Linnie's feet. They wagged themselves all over. They whimpered at the edge of the cereal bowl. Bess slid part way into it and had to be lifted out, with her front paws milky.

"I hope you like cornflakes," Linnie said. She was down on her knees steadying their dinner so they wouldn't waste it. When the bowl was empty, she poured her glass of water into it and propped it between the rungs of a broken ladder that lay along one wall. Harry trotted around with his tail up, found the spot he wanted, and dampened the earth floor. Bess chased him and they rolled over twice, mouthing each other, not biting. They attacked Linnie's shoes, chewed the laces, pulled at her socks.

"Don't do that," she scolded, scooping one up in each arm, laughing, nosing their soft fur. "How am I going to explain chewed-up socks?" She shrieked when they found her hair and tugged at it. "Ow! Not so hard, please."

She put them down and sat cross-legged, beaming on their mischief. The afternoon sun beamed, too, right through the garage's dusty west window. Golden light filled the little building. Linnie was so happy that she was afraid to move. It was like having a jigsaw puzzle with the last piece just in, and not wanting anyone to jiggle the table. Or like being in the very best part of a good book and not wanting the end to come. She wondered if the birthday dog would be as perfect as Harry and Bess. How could she wait a week?

And then she remembered that no one knew where she was, and she hadn't any idea how long she had been sitting there. "Good-by," she said, and kissed each pup on the nose. They were too cute to have germs, no matter what Aunt Em thought. Then she squeezed out the door and around the back of the garage, across the lane and through the garden, where she looked for weeds among the seedlings just in case anyone was watching.

Hide and Seek

The next day the dogcatcher came around twice, looking for the strays. Darla stayed as close to Linnie as butter on bread, so there was no chance to check and see if he had found anything when he drove his old green truck up the lane.

Darla was bored. She didn't want to read, or play Old Maid or Rook or any of the other card games Linnie knew. She said she was tired of practicing for the program, and of hearing Linnie say her poem. She had brushed her hair so many times that Linnie was sure it would all fall out. She didn't talk much, but she wouldn't give Linnie a minute by herself.

After supper there was a little argument about what they would do, and Linnie won.

"Okay," Darla said grudgingly. "Hide-and-seek. But it's not going to be any fun with just the two of us."

"Sure it will." Linnie wanted to hurry. She had a pocketful of table scraps that were getting gooey. "You be It," she said, "and make sure you count clear up to a hundred."

Darla sighed and leaned her head against the side of the house and began counting.

"Can you see?" challenged Linnie.

Darla sighed again. "Eighteen, nineteen, twenty—"

Linnie scurried across the road. There wouldn't be time to play today. She let herself into the garage and took a long breath. Harry and Bess were both there, bouncing toward her like lumpy rubber balls. There was still a little water in the cereal bowl and some crumbs on a paper plate, which meant that Arnold had been there. Good for Arnold.

She emptied out her pocket. There were bread crusts with some of the jelly left on; a few bites of cheese; both halves of a chocolate chip cookie, a real sacrifice; and a tidy round bone from the middle of the pot roast. "Don't fight over it," she said and gave each one a scratch, longing to stay.

Then the door was flung open from outside. "There you are!" accused Darla.

Linnie sucked in her breath. "You must have cheated," she said. "You peeked. You wouldn't have found me."

"Huh." Darla tilted up her head. "You were just trying to get away from me. I could tell."

"Oh, bananas," said Linnie, borrowing from Arnold. "Shut the door, then, so they don't get out."

But Bess was already on her way, sniffing along the ground, trotting straight toward Darla's feet.

"Close the door!" commanded Linnie, trying not to shout.

Darla looked down. "Oh," she said.

"Close the door," hissed Linnie again. "Arnold has to keep them here so the dogcatcher won't get them while he's finding them a home."

"Oh," repeated Darla, staring as the pup came toward her.

"Well, pick her up, then," urged Linnie, trying to get a hand on Harry to keep him from going out, too. "Do something. She's going to get away, for heaven's sake."

Darla closed her eyes and bit her lip and thrust out her right foot. It caught Bess in the hindquarters and sent her tumbling with a *yip! yipe!*

Linnie's mouth came open all by itself. "You kicked her!" she said. "You kicked that poor little dog." Her stomach didn't have a bottom. How could anyone—? She dropped to her knees beside Bess.

"I didn't!" Darla said. "I just put out my foot to keep it from getting away." Her hands fluttered up to her hair and down again without touching it. She swallowed. "I don't know what you're doing over here, anyway."

"Just checking," Linnie said. "Just making sure they aren't going to starve or anything."

Bess shook herself and wobbled to her feet and began to climb over Linnie's knee as if nothing had happened.

"There, see?" said Darla, back to her regular voice. "It's all right. Let's go back."

"I guess we'd better," Linnie said. She put both of the puppies into their cardboard and paper nest, although she knew it would not hold them for more than a minute or two. Then she saw to it that the door was shut and that the trampled grass was fluffed up a little.

"We have to keep this place a secret," she said. She thought about Bess whining from the sting of Darla's toe, and her feelings got the better of her good manners. "You'd better not tell," she said. "If you do, I'll—I'll throw your old baton in the creek or something."

Darla squinched up her mouth as if it had a draw-string on it. "Well," she said. "What a fuss. They're just dogs."

Linnie kept herself from saying anything, but she thought plenty: Darla Gayle Champion was the most stuck-up, disgusting, insensitive, boring, rotten person she had ever known.

"Amidst the storm they sang...."

On picnic day Linnie disgraced herself. She was grouchy to begin with, because of Darla and because of the poem she had to recite. It kept fading out of her mind. She didn't like it, anyway, because it was a Thanksgiving poem, all wrong for the middle of May. When she had complained to Miss Crane, the teacher had clucked her tongue and told her it was a perfectly good poem for any season, thank you, and Linnie should take care to render it with feeling and not as if she were reading from a bread wrapper.

"'The breaking waves dashed high,'" muttered Linnie, trying to remember, "'On a stern and rockbound coast. And the—while the—' Rats!"

Grouchy or not, she had to walk to the schoolhouse with Mom and Aunt Em and Darla. Dad was at work and Granpop never went to picnics. Garrett had gone on ahead with his friend David Ray Allen, who had graduated the night before and said he was going to join the Navy, so Garrett was trying to spend every minute with him that he could. Linnie carried a box of ham sandwiches and pretended to be happy. It was, after all, the last day of school and less than a week till her birthday.

"My, but it's hot for this time of year," Aunt Em said, stopping to fan herself with one of their paper plates before they were halfway there.

"I hope it doesn't storm," Mom said. "The air feels like it might."

Linnie looked at the sky, which was hazy. "It won't," she said, hoping.

Darla didn't say anything. She just twitched along the side of the road with her baton and a sundress over her costume so she wouldn't have to change at school.

Linnie pushed at her hair. The humid weather made it turn every which way, no matter how hard she brushed it. Her new checkered dress was too hot; she wished it didn't have any sleeves. She almost wished that she could wear a costume like Darla's, even though she had heard Aunt Em going on to Mom about how shameful it was to let a child show that much of her behind right in public. Darla was going to be the coolest thing at the program, that was sure, with her arms and legs bare all the way.

But the picnic came first, and Linnie wanted to enjoy it, Darla or no Darla. Long tables were set up in the gymnasium, making one end of the huge room a marvel of meat loaves and sandwiches, deviled eggs and carrot sticks, pickles and bananas and strawberry gelatin and brownies and pies and good things of every kind. Even the smell was wonderful, Linnie thought, shifting from one foot to the other as the two serving lines moved slowly toward the food. She waved at Sally Maloney, hoping that Sally would save a place for her to sit. But Sally's line was the faster one, and she went off to eat at one of the back tables with Teresa Finney and two third-graders.

Darla didn't seem to want to go squeeze in beside them, so Linnie had to stay with her, at a table full of grownups, with nothing to do but eat.

Sally's mother sat next to the McKays and kept saying, "Have you tried Mrs. Anderson's salad? Did you get any of this cake? Do you think it's oil she uses, Jane, instead of butter? Is that what it is?" Linnie's middle felt tighter and tighter, because it seemed only good manners to try all those things that Mrs. Maloney recommended.

"You, too, sweetheart," Sally's mother said over and over to Darla. "Have some."

Darla kept saying "No, thank you" with her see-how-polite-I-am smile.

"Isn't she the skinniest little thing!" Mrs. Maloney said, just as if Darla weren't there. "So pretty!"

Linnie excused herself. She went to the corner table and got some fruit punch and then drank it alone, up near the stage where the high school boys were setting up folding chairs for the program.

The sun had gone under, dimming things a bit. A used napkin blew from the top of an overflowing trash can. One of the double doors that opened to the outside lost its prop and banged shut.

"Feel that air!" said someone's grandmother, fanning herself with a handkerchief. "What a relief." Linnie made her way around tables and chairs and went to the door for a look.

On the other side of the playground, a newly planted field sloped up and leveled itself off against the great spreading cloud on the horizon. Earth and sky were nearly the same color, except for the raggedy wisps of gray that raced overhead like heralds: storm coming! storm coming! Linnie swallowed hard and turned back to the inside. There was thunder, too, although it was hard to hear it over the sounds of chairs banging and dishes being put back in baskets and little brothers and sisters yelling.

Help, thought Linnie. Maybe she would be all right if she couldn't hear it. Maybe she could pretend it wasn't there. She went back to Mom and Aunt Em and stood close, while Darla was chattering away with Miss Crane about her dancing and her baton-twirling, and yes, she had her record with her. Garrett had already put it on the record player. She was all set.

"You, too, Linnie?" asked Miss Crane brightly. "Let's line up with the others, then."

A long, deep rumble of thunder came from the outside in, like a giant coming to the picnic with his empty belly growling. Linnie's face went white as library paste.

"What's wrong with you?" asked Darla. "You aren't sick, are you? You aren't going to throw up, are you?"

Aunt Em patted Linnie's shoulder. "She's all right," Aunt Em said. "Just go up there and speak your piece, child."

"Storms make Linnie a little nervous," Mom said.

"Oh." Darla nodded. "That. I used to be afraid, too, when I was younger."

Miss Crane beckoned. "Hsst! Come along." The first-grade rhythm band was already lined up on the stage, ready to go.

Clickety-click went the rhythm sticks as Mrs. Hughes struck the first notes of a march on the piano. *Rattle, rattle* went the castanets and tambourines, and a triangle pinged at random. Everyone who was in the program, about a dozen children in all, marched up to take their places at one side of the stage.

Linnie concentrated on her feet. She tried not to see the windows, which were high on the walls, almost to the gym roof. The noise of the rhythm band was a comfort, but then it stopped. The thunder lasted longer than the clapping. Linnie sat as still as she could, but her body wanted to move, to curl up somewhere dark and warm and safe. She twisted her fingers and played with the bow on the pocket of her dress while two third-graders sang a duet and Sonny Shoemaker played his accordion and the rain did its own dance and drum act on the flat roof above them.

Flash! *One-one thousand, two-one thousand.* A toddler started to howl and was taken into the hallway. *"The breaking waves dashed high,"* Linnie thought desperately, trying to block the real storm out of her mind. *"Not as the conqueror comes, They the true-hearted came. . . ."*

Darla sat in the chair beside her with the sundress still covering her costume, peaceful as a Sunday School picture. She gave Linnie half a smile.

"And now," Miss Crane announced, almost shouting to be heard, "we'll hear from Linnie McKay. Don't forget to speak up, dear."

By some miracle Linnie's rubber legs carried her to the apron of the stage. There was lightning again, and quicker thunder.

" 'The Landing of the Pilgrim Fathers,' " she pronounced, "by—by Mrs. Felicia Hemans." Her tongue had turned to cotton.

"Louder, please," called Miss Crane.

Linnie clenched her hands at her sides and began. " 'The breaking waves dashed high. . . .' " The words came out of her like water out of a pitcher, without thought. Her mind was on other things. I'll die, she thought. She had a picture of herself with a lightning bolt through the heart, a neat-edged comic-book zigzag. The next thunder-clap shook the windows. She couldn't get her breath.

" 'Amidst the storm they sang,' " she panted, " 'And the stars heard, and the sea. . . .' "

At that moment it came, the flash and the roar at once. A crackle of blue surprised the eye and stunned it; the ceiling lights went out without flickering, like snuffed candles. The sound was painful, like being too close to the fireworks on July Fourth.

Linnie screamed and ran down off the stage into the audience, to her mother, and clung to that safe shoulder, whimpering. Like a baby, Linnie thought afterward, ashamed. Just like a baby.

Granpop's Discovery

Darla reigned over the supper table, beaming.

Mom said, "She was just wonderful, Andy," and Garrett told the story to Dad and Granpop twice, with more details the second time.

"After the lightning struck the pole and knocked out the transformer," Garrett said, "and everything stopped—" He paused and looked across at Linnie. "After that, it was Darla's turn, but the record wouldn't play, of course, since there wasn't any power. So she got right up there in front of everybody and said 'Just a moment, please, ladies and gentlemen,' and went down to the piano and found out what Mrs. Hughes could play."

"It wasn't my regular music at all," Darla put in. "I had to adjust the routine and everything."

"It looked as if you'd practiced it for months," Mom said. "It was smooth as could be."

Garrett chuckled. "It was the costume that really got 'em," he said to Darla. "When you went behind the edge of the curtain and stepped back out in that little red suit and all those seventh- and eighth-grade boys started to whistle—"

"If it was me," Aunt Em said, "I'd lengthen that skirt by a good four inches."

"Now, Em," Mom said.

"She saved the show, all right," Garrett went on. "It's a good thing someone did." He looked at Linnie again.

Linnie was trying not to listen. Darla this, Darla that, Darla something else. No one had mentioned the final report card that Miss Crane had given Linnie with all its rows of neat little A's, like tents on a campground.

"Darla ought to try out for the Amateur Hour," said Garrett. "That's what Mrs. Elliott said, anyway. You know, the new teacher that did all the plays this year."

Mom's eyes crinkled as she smiled. "Wouldn't that be exciting, Darla? Did you ever think about that?"

"Oooooh." Darla's smile glittered. "That's my dream, to be on television. Or in the movies. Or be like a Rockette, at Radio City Music Hall, in New York City. We went there once."

Bragger, Linnie thought, and counted the uneaten peas on her plate: three, eight, nine, fourteen. They were canned peas, with horrible gray-green insides that mushed up in your mouth like something rotten. Ugh.

"I need to be excused," she said, and went out on the back step. For some air, she told herself.

"Too much picnic?" she heard Dad ask, back at the table.

"Too much something," Mom said, and the way she said it made Linnie feel worse.

"That was an awful storm," Aunt Em put in. "I came near to jumping out of my skin when it struck."

"Yessir," came Granpop's voice, agreeing. "I was over

in the garden when it started and I thought sure I was in for a soaking."

"You got home before you got wet, didn't you?" Mom asked, all concerned. She was always telling Granpop not to catch cold.

"Oh, I took care," he said. "I waited it out in Jack Tramp's old garage."

No! Linnie forgot about the flash of lightning that had undone her, and the flash of Darla Gayle Champion's baton. She tuned her ears to the kitchen, and held her breath till it hurt.

"For heaven's sake," Aunt Em was saying. "I suppose the inside is in as bad a shape as the outside, with no one ever taking care of it."

Please don't tell, Granpop. Please don't, Linnie thought, trying to send the message from her mind to his.

Granpop cleared his throat, and she heard his cup clank down into its saucer. "Looks about the same as it always did, I guess."

Then Darla's voice: "Oh, did you notice—?"

Linnie bit her lip so hard she tasted blood.

Darla seemed to be taking a swallow of something. "Did you notice how everyone clapped when I did the splits? That really surprised me. And they seemed to like that flip at the end." Her voice dropped and Mom's voice chimed in.

Linnie breathed again. Thank goodness that Darla was so stuck on herself she didn't have time to talk about dogs.

Granpop harrumphed and got up from the table. "Think I've got a peppermint in the cupboard," he said.

"I expect Linnie could use it." And in a moment he was outside with her and they were off to the orchard.

"Got to inspect my trees," he said, and went on in silence. The sun had come out in time to make a pinkish rim of clouds in the west. Everywhere birds were chittering. Under the apple trees last week's blossoms went on sinking into the long wet grass, with a hint of their old perfume. Linnie reached for Granpop's hand, feeling better.

"You'll never guess what I saw this afternoon," he said. Linnie looked up at him. She could tell by his face—he knew that she knew.

"Over in Jack's old garage," he went on, "I found two of the cutest pups you'd ever want to see. A male and a female. Brown and white, mostly. Couldn't say what kind. Pure mutt, likely. Maybe you'll want to sneak over and have a look at them, before the dogcatcher beats you to it."

"You wouldn't call him, would you?"

"Me? No, but that's no sign he won't get called somehow or other."

"Arnold's trying to find a place for them to live," Linnie explained.

"Arnold Anderson?" Granpop chuckled. "That boy reminds me of a flea. Wouldn't depend on him to remember his name, let alone take care of a dog. Every day when I find the paper, I think to myself, there's another miracle, pure and simple."

"Did they have enough food and stuff?" Linnie wanted to know.

"They do now." Granpop winked. "But don't tell Em."

"Oh, Granpop!" Linnie put her arms around his waist

and squeezed so hard that the rim of his pocket watch pressed against her cheek.

He patted her hair. "One of 'em—the little male—made me think of you, child," he said. "Shivered like a poplar tree during that storm. It's a wonder the little fella didn't wear himself out."

Linnie pulled away. "You mean he was afraid?"

Granpop nodded. "Scared to death, that's what it looked like to me."

How awful, Linnie thought. "Poor Harry!" she whispered, knowing the dread that must have filled his tiny chest.

"What's that?" said Granpop. "What's its name?"

"Harry," she said. "And the other one's Bess. Arnold named them."

Granpop's smile started as a crack in his face and widened to let a laugh come rolling out. "Harry and Bess!" he said. "Harry and Bess!" He couldn't seem to stop laughing. "Go on with you," he said. "Go around by the garden and look in on them. It'll do you both good." He shook his head. "Harry and Bess," he said again.

Linnie went. When she got her own dog, she thought, she would be sure not to name it after a President.

Biscuits

School was out and Linnie's birthday was coming, and everything should have been wonderful. But instead, things were only so-so. Bad and good.

The bad part was Darla: Darla talk, talk, talking while Linnie was trying to read; Darla dancing and dancing so much that Granpop had to find an old piece of linoleum to protect the kitchen floor; Darla calling Mom "Auntie Jane" and Mom hugging her. Double ugh! thought Linnie, and went off by herself with a pencil and a Goldenrod tablet left over from school to write things that would make her feel better. But still Darla poked in so—"What are you doing, Linnie? Can't I see?"—that Linnie gave it up.

The good part was Jack Tramp's garage. Even when Darla had to go along, which was almost every time, Linnie's visits with Harry and Bess were the best thing about the day. Arnold brought them food and water every morning, except for when it spilled out in his newspaper bag and people all along the route threatened to report him because their front pages were sticky.

Afternoons and evenings were Linnie's times, and Granpop helped her make excuses so that no one else would know. But he began to look a little worried about it. "They can't stay in that garage forever, child," he warned her one day.

"I know, Granpop," she said. 'Arnold's looking." But it seemed natural and right to have two dogs in Jack Tramp's garage, to play with them and bring their food and tidy up their floor.

"Phew," Darla said when they went into the garage. "It stinks in here."

"Does not." Linnie always held her breath a moment until she got used to the air. "If they could go outside, it would be different."

Arnold had managed to get away from home after supper, since his father had almost forgotten there had ever been a problem. Arnold was helping Linnie clean up and put some more papers in what was left of the box where the puppies slept.

"They're good dogs," he said, squatting down to call them into his lap for a treat. "Good old doggie. Here, Harry! Biscuit! Look at that, Linnie. Look at him chew. Come on, Bess. Get your biscuit, girl. I had enough trouble buyin' these without Roger Fiddler up at the store askin' a whole bunch of questions. They were for a friend, I told him, and then he wanted to know was it a four-legged friend. Some comedian."

Darla perched on one end of the ladder that lay propped against the side of the garage. "They aren't old enough for biscuits," she said. "It's probably going to ruin their stomachs or something. It might even kill them."

"No, sir!" Arnold frowned. "They *like* biscuits. Look at 'em attack."

Linnie worried. Her forehead got wrinkles. What did

Arnold Anderson know about puppies' digestive systems anyway? In school he had drawn a diagram of human insides with the lung connected to the large intestine.

"Arnold," she said, "maybe we ought to save the biscuits until Harry and Bess are a little older. What if they get sick? We'd have to tell somebody then, and you know what would happen."

"Aw, bananas." Arnold reached into the box and took out another biscuit and bit into it himself. "See there?" he said, crunching. "They're perfectly safe."

Darla shrieked and turned her face away.

Linnie giggled. "Arnold," she said, "you spit that out right now. That's dumb. You aren't a dog."

He got down on all fours then and wiggled his bottom half and started to bark, with biscuit crumbs dribbling out of his mouth. The puppies jumped on him and chased their own tails, yipping and yapping like squeeze-toys. Linnie started to laugh because he looked so ridiculous. Finally she had to sit down, and then the puppies went after her. They climbed into her lap and took mouthfuls of her long hair and shook it.

"Ouch! Yow!" By the time they all settled down, she and Arnold were breathless, as empty as used balloons.

"That's disgusting," Darla said. "People who have dogs don't get down and act like dogs themselves."

"How do you know?" challenged Arnold. "Did you ever have one?"

"No," she said. "I wouldn't want one."

"That just proves what a dumb cluck *you* are," said Arnold.

Attaboy, Arnold, thought Linnie, but she kept her face

straight. She drew Harry up close to her, nose to nose. He was warm and fat and round in her hands; his eyes were alive with what to do next.

"Why not, Darla?" Linnie asked. "Why wouldn't you want a dog?"

Darla got up slowly and tucked her blouse inside the waistband of her pedal pushers. "I wouldn't have time to take care of it," she said. "I'm much too busy with lessons and practicing and everything."

"You can do all that stuff already," Arnold said. "Everyone at school was real impressed. What do you want to keep on taking lessons for?"

Darla sniffed. "You wouldn't understand," she said. She started for the door. "Come on, Linnie. Let's go."

Linnie was still cuddling Harry. "*I* want a dog," she said. "And I'm getting one, I think. I hope. For my birthday. Monday."

Darla turned around. "I bet you aren't," she said. "Your Aunt Em doesn't like dogs at all. She thinks they're worse than a nuisance, that's what she told me."

"She'd get used to it," Linnie said. "I know she would. But don't you say anything about it, either of you. There's supposed to be some kind of surprise, and I've heard things—"

Darla said, "Hmph. I bet it isn't a dog."

But Arnold's face lit. "Yeah!" he said. "That would be great. If you got a dog, then I could pet it and everything but I wouldn't have to take care of it."

"Sure, Arnold, you old lazy thing." Linnie put Harry down and followed Darla. "I promise. If I get a dog you can play with it."

If, if. She was beginning to feel sure of it. Just the night before, she had heard bits and pieces of talk from downstairs, voices through the register.

"It will be good for everyone in the long run," Mom had said. "You'll see, Em."

Then Aunt Em, halfway between cross and something else: "Not for me it won't. I don't know if I'll ever be able to—" Then something loud on the radio covered their voices, just before Linnie drifted off to sleep.

"Come on home with us, Arnold," she said now, feeling good. "We'll listen for the birthday ghost, the way we did last year."

Darla made a delicate snorting noise. "That sounds pretty boring to me," she said.

"Huh," said Arnold. "Everything we do sounds pretty boring to you, I guess."

She turned and gave him a dazzling, sweet, on-stage smile and didn't say a word.

Ghost Story

As far as Linnie knew, the birthday ghost was real. But Darla wouldn't believe a word of it when Linnie told the story; the three of them had to find Granpop so that Darla could ask for herself.

Granpop was in the front porch glider, snoozing behind yesterday's paper.

"There isn't really a ghost in this house, is there?" Darla asked while Granpop blinked and pretended to have been awake all along.

"No," he said. "No such thing."

"Hah!" crowed Darla in Linnie and Arnold's direction. "There! I knew better."

Granpop blinked again. "Unless you count that fool business about the footsteps."

"Tell her," said Linnie, feeling smug. "She wouldn't believe *me*."

"Yeah," said Arnold. "Tell it. I like ghost stories."

"Oh, I wouldn't call it a ghost story," Granpop said. "Probably a fellow could explain it if he just knew where to start."

"What happened?" Darla asked. She looked almost interested.

Granpop pulled Linnie down beside him and the glider rocked a little, gentle as a cradle. The rightness of everything settled around her: the scent of the lilacs, the roughness of Granpop's shirtsleeve, the words of his story. It was all familiar and dependable and good.

"The night Linnie was born," Granpop said, "right here in this very house—"

"I thought babies were born in hospitals," interrupted Darla. "I was."

Granpop nodded. "Oh, I expect you were. That's the way of it in the big places, I know that. And here too, now, almost always. But back before the war, there were a good many babies born at home, with just the doctor and someone to help out, usually. Em was here for Linnie's mother."

Arnold moved in closer to Granpop. "What did she do to help?" he asked.

Granpop rubbed one ear. "I'm not so good at details like that," he said. "One thing was, she made lemonade and gave a big glassful to the doctor when it was all over. I know that much."

Linnie saw the disappointed look on Arnold's face, and understood it. That wasn't what Arnold wanted to know.

"She was born about noontime, this little one," Granpop went on. Linnie's cheeks reddened. She didn't mind being called "this little one"; what she minded was having Darla hear it.

"And then the doctor said it was a good job and went on back to his other calls and we all had a look at her. Garrett said—you remember, now, he wasn't very old at the time—he said she looked like a wrinkled tomato."

Linnie made a face while the other two giggled. Why did he have to tell that part?

"When it came night," Granpop said, "there was Jane and the baby in the downstairs bedroom with Em to take care of them. And Andy and I and Garrett, we went upstairs to sleep where we'd be out of the way. Pretty soon, after midnight it was, Em comes up the stairs just a-huffin' and says 'You can quit your trompin' around up here. There's nothin' to worry about,' she says, 'so you don't have to pace back and forth like the devil was on your tail.'" Granpop stopped to rub his chin. "I'll tell you this, she woke us all out of a sound sleep. Not a one of us had been out of bed. But Em swore up and down she had heard footsteps back and forth across the upstairs. They came to the top of the steps, she said, and then waited like they might come on down, but then they'd turn and go back."

Darla's eyebrows arched up. "*This* upstairs, you mean?" she asked, pointing. "Where we sleep?"

Granpop gave a nod. "But don't you worry about it. I never heard a thing, and neither did Andy. Em's the one that heard it, and she'd had quite a day, remember."

"Mom heard it, too," Linnie reminded him. "She said so."

"Well, yes," Granpop agreed. "She heard something. But then, she'd had a hard day, too."

"Aunt Em didn't stay," prompted Linnie. "Tell that part."

"True enough," Granpop said. "She said she wasn't spending any night under the same roof where there were footsteps but no feet, and she went straight over home.

Andy had to hire a nurse from Springtown for the nights until Jane was up and around again."

"And Aunt Em's never spent the night here since, either," Linnie added.

"Nope," said Granpop. "But you know how Em is when she gets something into her head."

"Boy," said Arnold. "I wish I lived in a haunted house."

"Don't exaggerate, now," said Granpop. "It was just a funny, one-time thing."

Darla stood very straight and tossed her head so that her hair bounced across the top of her shoulders and settled back in its perfect curve. "I agree with you," she said to Granpop. "It was probably nothing."

Linnie sniffed. She didn't quite believe that the house was haunted. But it wasn't a "nothing." It was something. The story set her apart in a special way, like a birthmark.

Granpop gave Darla his slow smile. "Don't let these two try to scare you," he said, pointing at Linnie and Arnold.

"Oh, they won't." Darla's laugh came out like a trill on a toy xylophone.

Afterward, when Arnold and Linnie talked about keeping a vigil every night after sunset to listen for the footsteps, Darla was scornful.

"Can't you think of anything better to do?" she asked. "Couldn't we go to a movie or something? Or go into Springtown to that candy store? Couldn't someone take us in? I'd love to get some chocolate-covered almonds like I used to get in Pittsburgh. And it would be something to *do!*"

"We could go back and play with the pups," Linnie suggested. "That would be something to do."

"No," said Darla. "Not that." Her chin wobbled and then she took a deep breath and walked away from them, straight to the orchard, where she climbed the corner apple tree and sat looking up the street.

" 'Chocolate-covered almonds,' " mimicked Arnold, whispering. " 'Like Pittsburgh! Oh, I wish I had something to do!' Huh!" he said. "Chocolate-covered dog biscuit would be more like it. I'd be glad to make her some."

"Arnold!" Linnie cupped one hand over her mouth to keep the giggle from spilling out. "You wouldn't dare!" But somewhere inside her was a small, guilty hope: Maybe he would.

The Day of the Dogcatcher

The dogcatcher's name was Morrison Sparks, spelled out in square black letters on the door of his truck.

What's he doing here? Linnie said to herself when she saw him turn into Granpop's driveway. It was just after lunch on Saturday, a peaceful time. Dad and Garrett were at the shop, and Granpop had gone fishing with Roger Fiddler's father. Even Darla was away for the moment, at the post office.

"She's hoping for a letter from her folks," Mom had said to Aunt Em in a private voice. "She's getting homesick, I'm afraid. I do wish they'd write her."

Linnie wished so, too. She wished that Darla would get a letter that said *Dear daughter, We have found a new house and we want you to come at once. . . .* Anyway, Linnie was glad that Darla wasn't here right now. No telling what she might say to the dogcatcher.

Aunt Em stood at the back screen, and Linnie peered around her for a better look at the truck, which was a nasty pale green color, like overcooked vegetables. The sight of it made a cramp in Linnie's stomach; it was even worse than going to the dentist.

"What can we do for you, Sparks?" asked Aunt Em, holding her dishtowel so that he could see she was busy. Morrison Sparks was a great talker, and Aunt Em never liked to waste time.

"Just stopped by to show you what I had," he said. "Thought you could keep your eye out for the other one."

"The other what?" Aunt Em stepped outside and Linnie followed.

"Like to never found this one in the first place. Been looking all week. Somebody's been feedin' it, though. Thought it might have been you folks."

"What is it?" Aunt Em wrinkled her nose as she neared the truck. "A stray?"

"Just a little one. Cute, ain't it?"

Aunt Em peered through a wire mesh window, set high in the back of the truck. "Sure it hasn't got the mange?"

"Aw, Emma, don't be so persnickety." The dogcatcher laughed with such a deep gurgly sound that Linnie could have liked him if only he hadn't been the dogcatcher. "That's a perfectly healthy little dog if I ever saw one," he said.

"Mr. Sparks?" Linnie's voice squeaked. "Can I see?"

"Sure. Here, let me give you a boost." He put his wide rough hands under her arms and with an embarrassing little *umph* that showed she was heavier than he had expected, he lifted her even with the window.

There sat Bess, looking very alone, like half of something. When Linnie's head came into view the puppy twitched her nose and began to wiggle and whine.

Mr. Sparks set Linnie down. "She likes you, that pup

does. How about it, Emma? Want to take the dog for your girl here?"

Linnie opened and closed her mouth. Maybe, maybe—maybe this was how they had arranged it. Maybe the dog-catcher was really here to deliver the birthday dog. Maybe she could choose. Maybe—

"Indeed not, Sparks," Aunt Em said sharply. She rested her hand on Linnie's shoulder. "There's no place for a dog here."

"You don't know anything about this one, then?" He took off his cap and scratched his head. "I think it's one of the ones Anderson called me about last weekend. Found it just down the road apiece, drinking out of that little stream in George Fisher's pasture."

"I don't know anything about it," Aunt Em said, "and I don't care to, either. Got enough to think about without hearing the life story of some stray, I'll tell you that." She turned to go in.

"You haven't seen another one just like this, then? There was two of 'em."

"No," Aunt Em said. "I already told you. No dogs here, and I'm thankful."

"Maybe I ought to ask Leo," the dogcatcher said, rubbing his head.

Linnie closed her eyes and prayed that he wouldn't.

Aunt Em began to look cross. "Not worth your time," she said. "He'd have told me if he'd seen anything."

"Well, if you do find it, put it in your shed and give me a call," Mr. Sparks said to Aunt Em's back as she disappeared into the house.

"If I see it," she called, "I'll run it off. And then I'll call and let you know which direction."

The dogcatcher laughed. "She's somethin', your Aunt Emma," he said to Linnie.

Linnie bit her lip. Something was terribly wrong. Aunt Em didn't sound anything at all like a person who was going to get used to a dog by next Monday. And there sat Bess, crying in a cage, where she wasn't supposed to be, ever. How did she get out? Linnie wondered. And where was Harry? She wanted to jump up and rip the wire out of the back of the truck and clutch Bess and shout, "She's mine! She's mine! I'm keeping her!" But all she did was sniffle her nose.

"What's going to happen to that little dog?" she asked.

Mr. Sparks got into his truck and adjusted his cap. "Well," he said, "I don't think I'll have her too long."

"You mean you're going to—?" Linnie couldn't make herself say any of the things that people sometimes said, like "put her away" or "put her to sleep."

"No," Mr. Sparks said. "Not this one. There's a lady just the other side of Springtown wants a pup this size. I'll take it over there and see if this one will do."

Linnie felt a bubble of hope rise up through the sludge of misery that had settled in her chest. "Oh," she said, "I hope—"

The truck rattled into reverse, and she called good-by to Bess under cover of its noise. As soon as it was out of sight, she ran across the road and up the lane to Jack's garage.

Harry was still there. Alone and whining, but there, with a note from Arnold written on a page of classified ads and stuck on a nail under the window. BESS HAS EXKAPED. LOOS BORD I THINK. Linnie could see where he had made a tighter pile of scrap material and wedged it against the wall. The note continued: I WILL GO OUT AND SURCH FOR HER ON MY BIKE. A. A.

Linnie picked Harry up and loved him, dropping tears on his brown back. She wept for his loneliness and the loss of his sister, and for the dim garage that might seem like a cage to him. Who could tell? She wept because she couldn't take him outdoors and into the sunshine of the yard and up on her very own bed to sleep there as her very own dog. She wept for herself because Darla Gayle Champion was such a pain that she spoiled everything. She wept for the possibility that there might be just plain birthday presents this year, and no surprise. She wept because she felt like it, for as long as she dared. Then she had to leave Harry and go out red-eyed into the afternoon. And there was Darla, coming from the post office, with a letter flapping open in her hand.

"What's the matter with you?" asked Darla, staring at Linnie's nose. "You've been crying, haven't you?"

"So?" Linnie rubbed furiously at her eyes and her nose as if the evidence could be scrubbed away. "The dog-catcher got Bess," she said. "He took her away. But he thinks there's someone who wants her so he won't have to —you know."

Darla shrugged. "I don't know why you're blubbering, then," she said. "That's what you wanted, wasn't it? To find a place for them? He ought to have taken the other one, too."

"Darla!" Linnie was horrified. "That's a mean thing to say. What if he couldn't find any place for Harry to live? Then what would happen to him?"

"Hmp." Darla turned the letter that she held around

and around in her hands, tracing its edges with one finger. "What if Arnold doesn't find anywhere for him? What then? I don't think Arnold looks very hard, anyway. The dogcatcher might as well have him, Linnie." Her voice got louder. "Grow up a little, why don't you? I never saw such a spoiled baby. You scream when it storms and you don't ever *do* anything. Just play around or have your nose in a book. And you cry for things you can't have. Frankly, I don't know how Auntie Jane puts up with you."

Darla creased the letter like a fan, and jammed it into her pocket. "My mother would keep you busy," she went on. "She'd have you join the Girl Scouts or take piano lessons or learn to knit or something. Or swim. She wouldn't just let you mope around, I'll bet, even if you did live way out in the–" Suddenly Darla stopped talking. She swallowed whatever it was she was going to say next, took a deep breath, and walked away with quick little steps.

Linnie stood where she was, numb as a stubbed toe. A spoiled baby, was she? She might have cried again, but her tears were all used up. To herself she began to name the unspeakable things about Darla Gayle Champion: stuck-up, hateful, too proud, always right. She had even kicked Bess, Linnie remembered. She couldn't wait to talk to Arnold. He would understand. A pox on girls who kick dogs, she thought fiercely, and went to find him.

A Present for Darla

Suppertime brought so much confusion that no one seemed to notice either of the girls or the silence between them. Dad and Garrett came home late, after the rest of them had begun to eat, and Dad told Mom to get her good shoes on because they were going back to Springtown. Business, he said, and winked at her. Granpop got up and shaved and put some brilliantine lotion on his hair so that he could go along with them, while Aunt Em slammed cupboard doors harder than she had to and muttered at the dishpan. Garrett seemed to know all about everything, but he wouldn't say much.

"Just wait," he told Linnie. "You'll find out."

Linnie checked the calendar. Her birthday was only two days away. It must be the surprise that was causing this commotion. It had to be. She ate a jam sandwich for dessert and saw that Darla wasn't eating anything. Good, thought Linnie. Maybe she would shrink up and blow away. Then she thought about Harry being all alone. Would he cry when it was dark? Was he whining now? She began to look around the kitchen for some special tid-bit to ease his grief, but Aunt Em didn't cooperate.

"Don't be underfoot, girls," Aunt Em said. "Not tonight. I'm all out of kilter and I'm better off alone. Go take a walk or something. I don't care."

"Aunt Em," said Linnie, "you aren't sick, are you?"

"Of course I'm not sick." Aunt Em sounded as if she were talking to someone else, not Linnie. "I was never in better health in all my life. Good as I ever was. Does anyone listen when I tell them that?" She dumped all the silverware into the dishpan at once, letting it clatter as much as it would. "Go on, girls, go on."

Darla took her baton, but she didn't twirl it.

"Listen," said Linnie, "you can do what you want to, but I'm going to the garage."

Darla shrugged. "Suit yourself."

What happened to her old mean mouth? wondered Linnie, just as she saw Arnold coming down the street. He was on his bike and looking cheerful.

"Hi!" he said, giving the largest part of his smile to Darla. "You're the one I'm looking for." He took a small white sack out of his shirt front and handed it to her. "This is for you," he said. "My mother had to go to town and she just happened to be at the candy store, and, well– This is for you," he said again.

"Why, Arnold!" Darla opened the sack and peered in, with something like her regular smile. "Chocolates!" she said. "Thank you very much." Her eyelashes fluttered once. "Are they the hand-dipped kind?"

Arnold bobbed his head up and down with enthusiasm. "They sure are," he said. "Individually made. Freshest nut clusters you could want."

"Well, thank you," Darla said again and rolled up the

top of the sack. "I'll save them for when I'm really hungry." Then she gave a little sigh and opened the sack again. "I don't know what's happened to my manners," she said. "Would you like a taste?"

Linnie looked at Arnold, whose face was covered with messages. "No, thanks," she said. "They're all for you."

"Well," Darla said, "I hope they'll be as good as the ones Auntie Jane made for the picnic."

Linnie took another look at Arnold, who was already pedaling toward the garage. "I don't know," she said. "Hardly anyone makes candy as good as Mom." She didn't wait to hear whatever Darla was saying. She chased after Arnold, all the way into the garage, where she found him leaning against one wall in a helpless giggling fit.

"Arnold!" she accused. "You didn't—"

He couldn't talk. His head nodded up and down while he tried to get his breath. Water came out of the corners of his squeezed-tight eyes.

"Where did you get that candy?" Linnie demanded. "Your mother didn't buy it at any candy store, that's what I'll bet."

Harry trotted around their feet, springing up against Linnie's bare legs, yapping and begging for fingers to chew, or hair to shake, or just a pat. Anything. Linnie lifted him and settled him in the crook of her arm like a baby, where she could tickle the pink part of his belly and make him close his eyes. "Now, Arnold," she said, "you'd better tell me."

"I made 'em myself," he croaked. "Just the way you told me your mother makes peanut clusters, remember? First I melted up a plain old chocolate bar, and then I broke some dog biscuits in little pieces and dropped them in and—"

"Arnold, you didn't! You shouldn't have! I mean, what if—?" But she couldn't help laughing. She thought about Darla carefully opening the sack, and carefully lifting out a chocolate-covered dog biscuit, and carefully taking a dainty, tiny bite. It was too much. She howled. Her shoulders shook. Harry licked her nose and she didn't care.

"You shouldn't have done it, Arnold, really," Linnie said again, when she had breath enough to talk. "What if it makes her sick? She'll get us both in trouble."

Arnold straightened himself up, finally, face and all. "Aw, bananas," he said. "I think it's been a pretty good day. Bess got a home, maybe, and Darla got a present. And it was something they both deserved."

Later, when it was bedtime and Linnie saw the little white sack, unopened, on the windowsill where Darla had found room to put a few of her things, it seemed as if the joke ought to be over. I should tell her, Linnie thought. But then if she did, how could she explain it without a lot of hurt feelings? On the other hand, if she didn't warn Darla and Darla bit into one of those things and then went running to Mom or Aunt Em or anybody, there would be a real fuss.

Linnie flopped over in bed, avoiding Darla's still form, and put her mind on other things. Mom and Dad and Granpop had come home from Springtown full of secrets. Tomorrow was surprise day, Mom had told her. A day-before-birthday present, too good to keep. She smiled in the dark. It could be a dog, maybe. There was still a chance.

It took a long time for Linnie to go to sleep, and then something wakened her. She lay without breathing, listening. Darla was crying—*unh, unh, unh*—with her face buried in the pillow. It was a soft, bad sound that made Linnie's own chin tremble. To hear someone sobbing in the night was almost as terrible as being the one who sobbed. Something inside her wanted to reach over and stroke the black hair and the hunched-up shoulder. Something inside her wanted to say comforting words. But she didn't say them. Linnie lay still and put on a stubborn face with no one to see it.

Who's blubbering now? she thought, nursing her own hurts. Just look who's blubbering now.

Surprise!

The surprise was in Springtown. Dad drove Granpop's car, with Mom beside him and Granpop by the window. The back seat held Garrett and Darla and Linnie, with plenty of room to breathe.

Aunt Em had refused to go. "I don't want anything to do with it," she said.

"Aunt Em, come on," begged Linnie. She was sure now, could almost feel the warm fur of her own dog in her own hands. "It'll be all right," she whispered. "I know it will." But Aunt Em wouldn't go.

Mom didn't coax. She hummed as if she were the one getting the surprise, and hurried them all into the car. "You could drive a little faster, Andy," she said.

Darla was herself again, chattering to Garrett and asking questions as the countryside bounced along outside the window: "What's planted in that field? How can you tell? What are silos for? What kind of chickens are those?"

On and on. Linnie sighed and leaned back against the seat, wide-awake dreaming. In her imagination she was running down Jack Tramp's lane with a needle-nosed collie at her heels, its shiny coat rippling the same as her own long brown hair. The picture changed, *click*, the way it did when you pushed the lever on Garrett's little slide viewer, the one that had a window for each eye. She was walking in fallen leaves, brown and gold, that just matched the curly ears of her spaniel. *Click*, again. There was a Scotty terrier like the one in an old picture book that she had loved, yapping at the barn cats, with its black chin whiskers wiggling. Then she told herself not to be silly. Her dog would probably be more ordinary, an everybody's dog. Like Harry. She thought about Harry, his stubby legs and flat white feet and the way he waddled across the floor of the garage to climb into her lap. She smiled to herself.

"Look at that," Garrett said, noticing the smile. "Linnie thinks she knows."

Darla lifted her chin. "And I know what she thinks, too," she said to Garrett. "I'll whisper it to you." She put her mouth right against his ear and said something that no one else could hear.

Garrett's jaw dropped and he looked at Linnie. "You're just plain out of your skull," he said.

Granpop turned one shoulder toward the back seat and started to say something, but at that moment the car stopped. They had come into Springtown without Linnie's noticing, and now they were in front of the tall cream-colored house where they had stopped last week. Bananas, thought Linnie, wishing that Dad would forget about his customers and get on with the surprise.

"Well, Rosebud," he said, getting out of the car and opening her door, "this is it."

Then she realized that this customer must be the one

with the dog. There must be puppies for sale here, or for giving away. She would get to choose, probably. Her neck was prickly with anticipation.

"Where?" she asked, stepping out onto the grassy space between the curb and the sidewalk.

"Right here," said Mom, sliding out of the front seat after Granpop. Her voice bubbled up out of her smile like fizz out of soda pop. "It's the house, Linnie! We're buying it. And for you there's the most wonderful bedroom. Really, wait till you see! It was someone's study once, with a window seat and a built-in desk and bookshelves. Perfect for your things, Lin. And there's such a good school, and—"

"We've already got a house, Mom." Linnie hung onto the car door. A vaguely sick, Ferris-wheel feeling rose and turned in her middle. "We live at Granpop's." She felt as if she were standing far away from the car and the house, looking on, watching someone else's life happen. She saw Darla's mouth form an *o*, saw Darla's face wrinkle up in delight, or envy.

"Oooooh, Linnie," Darla moaned. "You are so lucky. I'd love to live in a house like this. It's so—I don't know. And right in the middle of town, too. Oh, I wish it was me."

"We live at Granpop's," Linnie said again. "We've always lived at Granpop's."

"But if we didn't live at Granpop's," Mom said, "there would be more room for everybody. And Em would have a little peace and quiet without us underfoot all the time. She's wearing herself out taking care of us, Linnie. This is only two minutes from Dad's shop, so I can manage the house and the accounts besides, back and forth whenever

I need to be. With a little help from the rest of you, of course." She smiled from Linnie to Garrett and back again.

Dad put his arm around Mom's shoulders. "It's a honey of a place," he said. "Needs work here and there, but that's part of the fun of it. I've always wanted to try my hand at cabinets. . . ."

Linnie quit listening. Her mouth seemed to be all stuck together. She let her eyes slide off the house toward the one next to it, first one side, then the other. I can't live here, she thought. There were houses all up and down this street full of people she had never even heard of. She didn't know anyone. In Merrittsburg she knew every single person. She couldn't imagine living here, away from the apple trees and the barn and all the nooks and crannies of home, where even the floorboards had noted the day of her birth. What about Arnold Anderson? And Miss Crane? And everyone at school? How could she be away from Aunt Em and Granpop, who belonged with every day the way a sink belongs in a kitchen?

"Come on inside." Dad was tugging at her hand. "Just wait till you see this, Rosebud. It's huge. This way, Pop. You too, Darla."

Linnie felt herself move without wanting to, as if she were a wind-up toy with the key just turned. There were two steps up to the porch, with its fancy wood cutouts for trim. Opening from the porch was a double door with a lock, then an entryway not quite big enough for all of them at once, and then another set of doors, with frosty, see-through pictures in the glass. Finally they came into a hallway with a confusing number of rooms opening on either side. A stairway wound upward, with a banister curved like a swan's neck.

"Oh, how beautiful!" breathed Darla. "It *is* like a movie, I knew it." She went halfway up and then started back down, carrying herself like a princess, or a ballerina, with her toes pointed. Linnie thought of the stairs at home, plain and straight and dear to her, every step.

"It's a good house, Andy," Granpop said. He stood under the brass chandelier that hung from the lofty ceiling of the hall and rubbed his chin, studying the condition of the woodwork and the straightness of the walls. "It's a bargain," he said. "You can't even pay to get a house made as solid as this one nowadays."

To Linnie, his smile seemed a little crooked, lonesome, as if the family had already moved and left him. She went to stand beside him, but he just gave her head a little pat and bent to examine a crack along the baseboard.

"Listen," said Garrett, "I'm going down to measure that basement room and see how big a workbench it'll take." He started off down the hallway, whistling, and his feet made great thumping echoes in the empty house. Like thunder, Linnie thought with a shiver. She wanted to close her eyes and stop up her ears and wait for this storm to wear out and blow away.

But that wouldn't work. She had to go on the tour with her parents, looking into every room and closet, checking the view from every window. All bad, she thought miserably. To the front was the street and the swoosh of cars. To either side the windows were surprisingly close to other people's windows. Linnie had a glimpse of a man with his shirt unfastened, reading the Sunday paper. It made her blush; he had hair all the way down his chest and across his stomach, right to his belt.

Mom didn't seem to be bothered. She reached to the side of the window and drew a wooden shutter across the lower half of it. "We'll keep this part closed," she said, winking at Linnie. "There's plenty of light from the top."

Afterward, what Linnie remembered best was the kitchen, a long room that stuck out at the back of the house with its own porch, like a balcony, and a brick terrace below. The yard sloped down from there to a wood fence at the back, behind a garden all grown to weeds and an unexpected amount of grass.

Her own room-to-be was right above the kitchen, with a view that looked down toward green and out toward blue; that's how high it was. If she had been brave enough to stretch herself out the end window, she might have touched the leaves of a sycamore tree.

"I love it," Darla kept saying. "It's the best house. I hope my parents get one just like it."

Linnie wished that they could have this one. Or, better yet, that she could trade it for a dog.

Welcome Home, Harry

She buried her face in Flat Mabel's flat stomach and grieved. What a baby, part of her thought, but the rest of her didn't care, because there was no one to see. Darla had gone down to the cellar with Garrett so that he could show her how much better things would be in his new workshop. Everyone else was in the kitchen having a grown-up fuss, one that was Linnie's fault.

Mom's voice drifted up from below, upset, tight. "I thought she'd be so excited."

"I knew she wouldn't." That was Aunt Em. "I knew it. I told you so."

Then Granpop: "She'll come around. She'll be just like a broody hen in her own nest before you know it. Just wasn't expecting it, that's all."

"Maybe we shouldn't have tried to surprise her," Mom was saying. "It was only that I didn't want to get her hopes up about all that space and then have to—"

"Maybe you shouldn't be moving at all, that's what I think. It's a pity to upset everything and make a lot of trouble when we've always got along fine this way."

"Don't get started on that, Em," Dad said. "You know

how long we've thought about it and how much we've talked about it and all the reasons. Jane and I need a place of our own, and the kids are growing up. You shouldn't have to work so hard for us. Things change, Em. It's not as if we were going to be far away or anything like that. We'll be seeing you and Pop a lot. And it's all settled now, anyway, down payment and everything."

"Don't you go on and on to me, Andy McKay," Aunt Em snapped. "If you don't need me, you don't need me. No one has to hit me over the head to make me see that!" There was a scuffle of footsteps, and then the back screen slammed. Aunt Em's shoes crunched down the drive and clicked across the road toward her own house.

"Stubborn woman." Granpop's voice rose out of the silence. "Always was. She knows it's the best thing, I think, but she just can't give up and admit it."

"I'll go talk to her," Mom said. There was another jumble of talk, lower pitched. Then the door slammed again, and Linnie saw all three of them going toward Aunt Em's.

Sniffling, she fluffed up Flat Mabel's petticoat and put the rag doll back on her bookcase. It wasn't much comfort any more. For comfort, a person needed something alive.

"All I wanted was a dog," Linnie heard herself say. "If I just. . . ." The thought finished itself in silence: If I just had a dog.

But she did have a dog, in a way. There was still Harry. All at once it came to her that he must have had a miserable day, too, without Bess to keep him company. At first she intended only to check on him, to see if he had water and let him know that he wasn't forgotten. But then when she was actually there, in the garage, and Harry was giving her wet puppy kisses, working on her tear stains, she knew that it had to be more than that. She couldn't just shut the door and go away and leave him there, alone. Not when he was the only one who cared how she felt; she could see that in his eyes and in the way he tilted his head when she spoke to him.

Harry thumped his tail gently against her arm. She wanted to keep him so much that it was almost a real ache, like the flu. She held him and crooned nonsense in his ear. When he got wiggly, they played at tug of war with a stick, and tickle games, and other entertainments in which Harry was an acrobat and a clown and even the President himself, with a well-chewed cardboard desk. It was fun. Being with Harry was almost enough to make a person forget a day of bad surprises.

What if he could have been my dog? she thought. What if we could have stayed at Granpop's and Harry had come to live with us? She had a sudden urge, a hunger, to know what that would have been like. Impulsively, she tucked the puppy inside her shirt and carried him outdoors, where he blinked in the strong light. Across the road she went, in the front door, up through the empty house to the clutter of her room.

"Here we are, Harry," she said, pretending. "Welcome home." She plopped him down on the braided rug beside her bed and watched him waggle off, sniffing. He dribbled at the corner of the bookcase and she had to snatch him up and get some tissues.

"Naughty Harry," she said, but it was hard to scold him when he already looked so apologetic. What was a person supposed to do, she wondered, when a dog went all over the floor? Some dogs were very well behaved indoors, she knew that. "Just don't do it again, Harry," she warned, rubbing his ears, "or I'll have to—" But she didn't know what, and suddenly she was close to tears again.

She put him on the end of the bed and he stayed, curled up plump as a dumpling, the way she had always pictured a dog of her own. But Harry wasn't going to be her dog. The bed wasn't even going to be her bed any more. She let her expression crumple, getting ready to cry, but then she caught her breath instead, listening.

Someone was downstairs. From the sound of it, everyone was downstairs. Even Aunt Em.

"Linnie!"

"Coming!" Her face went red and pink and red again. "Listen, Harry," she whispered, jerking the dog off the bed, "you've got to stay up here until I can get you out of the house." But where was there to put him so that he wouldn't do his damages or follow her down the stairs?

"Linnie!"

"Okay!"

There wasn't time to think about the right place. She carried him to her parents' closet, which was less cluttered than hers, set him down with a pat, and propped the door with a stack of books so that he would have enough air. "Shhhh!" she whispered, and hurried downstairs to make sure that no one would be coming up to get her.

A Dog in the House

Mom was calling Linnie into the kitchen because her birthday cake was there. "I know it's early," she said with a determined smile, "but I thought we needed a little celebration today. And besides, the cake's best when it's fresh."

On a signal from Dad, they all sang. Aunt Em looked, and sounded, sour as a pickle; but she sang. Darla danced. She did a little clog step around the table and the lighted cake to the rhythm of "Happy Birthday."

Show-off, thought Linnie, but the sight of the cake cheered her up. Birthdays, at least, were dependable; you had one every year no matter where you lived.

"Happy birthday to you-oooooo-oooooo." The last note of the singing died away on an odd, quavering echo.

"Hey, Darla," said Garrett, "I didn't know you were a ventriloquist, too. Do that again."

"I didn't do anything," Darla protested. "Honest."

"Hush, you two," Mom said. "Linnie has to close her eyes and make a wish and blow these candles out before anyone gets fed."

"Get on with it, Rosebud," said her father. "I'm starved."

Linnie closed her eyes and wished for Harry to shut up. Then she blew as hard as she could. The tenth candle flickered but didn't go out.

"One more time," Granpop said. "And just count your lucky stars you don't have all *my* candles to blow out."

Mom handed Linnie the cake knife. "Don't worry, Lin," she said softly. "Everything's going to be all right. It'll be fall before we get the new house ready to move into, and you'll feel different about it by then."

Linnie tried for a smile. "Maybe," she said.

"By then everyone will be used to the idea, I hope," Mom said, looking from Linnie to Aunt Em.

Aunt Em bustled up out of her chair. "I'm going to make me some tea," she announced. "Settle my nerves."

Linnie began to saw down through the cake, taking care not to squeeze the top and bottom together into an angel-food sponge.

Shump, thwump.

She thought she heard something upstairs, a muffled thudding. She dropped the knife on an empty plate with a satisfying clatter.

"Oops!" she said, and tried to think of more things that would make enough noise to cover the noise upstairs.

Aunt Em cocked her head to one side. "What's that?" she said. "Shhh."

Everyone went perfectly quiet. Linnie didn't dare rattle the dishes. *Sliiiiide, shump.* What's he doing? Linnie thought frantically. She tried to think of something to do, but no ideas came.

Shump, wump . . . with painful slowness, *shump, wump* . . . toward the top of the stairs.

Aunt Em's face had turned white as paper. "My stars!" she whispered.

Darla's eyes were round and dark and unblinking, all stretched out of shape. "What is it?"

"Just don't get excited," Dad said, but he didn't get out of his chair.

Thud! on the top step. Granpop frowned and Garrett began to look nervous. *Thud!* coming down.

Aunt Em put her hands to her throat. "After all these years," she breathed. "Who would have thought it, after all these years?"

Thud, thump-thud-thump-thud-thump-thud, all at once, to the foot of the stairs. Darla screamed like a steam whistle.

"Ghost!" she cried. "It's the walking ghost!"

Dad got up.

"Don't go in there, Andy," Mom said.

And then Aunt Em squawked out a hoarse little scream of her own as she pointed toward the dining room door.

The ghost wagged his tail proudly. Puffs of closet dust decorated his ears and his snout and one front foot.

"It's a wild animal!" Aunt Em cried. "Oh, dear Lord, look at the foam! It's got the rabies!" She made a lunge for the broom. Linnie made a lunge for Harry, but missed.

"Get back, child!" Aunt Em yelled, while Granpop tried to soothe her.

Harry ran under the table, lost his footing on the linoleum, and slid out again between Darla's feet. Darla stood up on her chair and closed her eyes, moaning.

"It's a dog, Emma," Granpop said, "just a dog." But by then Aunt Em wasn't listening. She was chasing, flailing.

Dad got up. "I'll catch it!" he shouted, and crouched beside the stove, waiting to grab as the pup came by. Garrett jumped up, too, whistling. The dog ran faster, dodging hands and feet and furniture.

"Harry!" cried Linnie, taking up the chase. "Come here, Harry!"

"Harry?" echoed Darla, as her eyelids flew up. "Harry?!"

"Yes," Linnie wailed. "It's just Harry." She stopped and pointed through the dining room doorway. "See Dad's old Army boot in there? That must've been what he was pulling down the stairs."

Mom's face wasn't pale any more. "Linnie," she said, "what's going on here?"

At that moment Aunt Em's broom caught Harry's bottom squarely from behind, and she swooshed him across the back porch and out the door. He landed with a yip and ran. Linnie flew down the back steps after him.

"Harry!" she called. "Come back!" But she had only one glimpse of him, streaking away across the road and disappearing into the tall grass.

Garrett followed Linnie into the yard. "Look at that little sonofagun go!" he said with admiration. Linnie covered her face with her hands.

"Aw, Linnie–" He adjusted his expression to a slow frown. "Am I going to have to go after him for you?"

Linnie took a giant breath. "Please," she said.

"Sisters!" Garrett pronounced, and loped off in the direction that Harry had gone.

After that, a lot of things happened at once. Linnie had to go inside and explain to her mother that Harry was

Arnold's dog, or at least he had been. Then she had to apologize to Aunt Em for bringing a stray into the house. Aunt Em insisted on calling Morrison Sparks right away, at home, so that he could get the earliest possible start on his work in the morning.

Darla said she couldn't get her breath and had to lie on the couch with a wet cloth on her head. "I'm just a little woozy," Darla kept saying. "I'll be all right in a minute." But she went on lying there, looking delicate as a china cup, and Linnie had to sit with her until she felt better.

By the time Linnie was free to go after Harry, Garrett had come back empty-handed, shaking his head.

"Sorry, Linnie," he said. "No sign of a pup anywhere." He shrugged and went back to his tubes and wires in the cellar.

Where, Oh Where . . . ?

Aunt Em told Linnie to leave well enough alone. Even Granpop said that finding Harry now would be about as likely as finding a snowman in July.

"You might as well go look, though, Linnie," her dad said. "You won't be satisfied any other way, now that you've got it in your head to worry about that dog."

Mom agreed that she could go, as long as she didn't go too far or stay too long. "It seems to me that Arnold ought to be the one to do the looking," her mother said, rubbing her head the way she always did when things had given her a headache. "It was his dog, wasn't it?"

But even with Arnold helping, the search was useless. The sun fell, and shadows stretched themselves out to cover everything. Twilight made every tuft of grass a tail, every bush a dog. Linnie was soon tired of whistling and calling and having all of Merrittsburg stare at her.

"What did you lose, child?" called Mrs. Darcy when Linnie poked along through the alley that lay between the Darcys' house and the post office.

"A little brown and white dog, a puppy. Have you seen it?"

Mr. Darcy came to stand at the kitchen window beside

his wife. "Not hide nor hair of it," he said. "I didn't even know you had a dog, Linnie."

"I don't," she said, and hurried to catch up with Arnold so that the Darcys wouldn't ask a lot of questions that she didn't feel like answering.

At the far edge of the school grounds, Arnold quit. "Bananaburgers," he said. "We might as well give up. Old Sparks is gonna get him for sure."

"Please, no," Linnie begged. It was all her fault, she knew. Why hadn't she left poor Harry in the garage where he would have been safe?

"We have to find him, Arnold," she said. "He's not used to being out all by himself. What if he gets run over? What if he catches pneumonia or something? Or what if it storms and he doesn't know where to go? Harry's afraid of storms, Arnold."

"Aw," said Arnold, unbelieving. "Dogs stay out in all kinds of weather. Some of 'em, anyway."

"Well, Harry shouldn't. We can't leave him out here," Linnie insisted.

"We can too," Arnold said. "We have to, because we can't find him. My father will skin me if I'm not home by dark. And it is, almost."

Linnie considered the sky and knew that she would have her own troubles if she didn't get back.

"I'll help look for him again in the morning, first thing," Arnold promised. "Maybe we can find him before Sparks does, anyway. But I don't know where we can put him this time."

Linnie's mouth drooped. "I don't know, either."

"It's hopeless," Arnold declared.

"Is not." Linnie's bottom lip stuck out far enough to show its pink inside. "Anyway, I want to see him one more time at least before he has to go in that awful cage. I have to say good-by, don't I?"

Arnold shrugged. "You act like he was your dog or something."

She sighed. "See you tomorrow, Arnold." Then her feet took her home, but her mind went on searching. Harry could be miles away by now, in Springtown even, although she wasn't sure how fast a puppy could travel. Or maybe he had circled around and come back into the bottom-land fields by the creek; the bank was so grown over that no one would ever find him there. He would starve to death probably and his tiny bones would be swallowed by mud. She wondered if he would turn into a fossil, or leave a picture of himself, like the shell prints Miss Crane had pointed out in a rock that Teresa Finney brought to school. He might even go as far as the Stones and scramble up to the ledge over the water, and fall, and drown.

Linnie shuddered. Please, Harry, she wished. Stay away from the creek. Also stay away from traps and chicken houses and big dogs and mean people. Take care of yourself, Harry. She trudged along by the post office, down the alley alongside Fiddler's Garage, and on toward Granpop's, thinking of Harry and how she would never see him again.

Then she thought of the house in Springtown. It could never be as good as home, with the apple trees on one side and the maples in front and that special, just-right look and feel of being the way home ought to be. She had to keep her eyes on her feet and try not to think.

Maybe she could sneak upstairs with a piece of birthday cake and stretch out on the rug beside her bed with a book. *Little Women* would be good, she thought, because she could go right to the chapter where Beth was dying and then if anyone asked about her red eyes she could just say "sad story" and not explain anything else.

But when she went into the kitchen, Mom was at the table making out bills for the repair shop, almost as if it had been a regular Sunday. "Any luck?" her mother asked.

Linnie shook her head.

"Well, don't worry so. From what I saw, it was a cute little pup. Whoever finds it will probably take good care of it."

Linnie tried to make her voice steady. "But I won't *know* that," she said. "I won't be sure."

Mom sighed. "I don't suppose it's any comfort, Linnie, but the sensible thing to do is forget about it. Put your mind on other things. Go upstairs and talk to Darla, for instance. She doesn't seem to be very happy today, either."

Linnie sighed, too. Her mother didn't understand. "What's the matter with Darla?" she asked. "Is it about the dog this afternoon?"

"That too, maybe, I don't know. But while you were gone, Bud and Marianna called to tell Darla they're all set and that she should come home day after tomorrow. They sounded so pleased about everything—"

"That's good, isn't it?" Linnie said, brightening. "She ought to be happy. I don't think she likes it very much, being here with me."

Mom looked at Linnie with one eyebrow up, and almost smiled. "Who is it that doesn't like it, I wonder?"

Linnie ducked her head and studied her fingernails.

"Anyway," her mother went on, "Darla barely said one word to any of us after they hung up. Just that she wished she could go back home, to Pittsburgh."

"Oh." Linnie felt a sudden twinge of kinship. Maybe Darla hadn't wanted to leave Pittsburgh any more than Linnie wanted to leave Granpop's.

"You're wishing you could stay put, too, I guess," Mom said, as if she could hear Linnie thinking. "But our new house is going to be just the thing for us—you'll see. That big room with the shelves and the desk and the window seat—did you even notice the window seat?—it was the best birthday present I could think of. Your dad thought we should use that room for an office, so I could do the shop accounts there, but I said no, that would be Linnie's library, and—"

"No," Linnie interrupted. "That's not the best birthday present. The best would have been a dog."

"But Linnie, what we thought was—" Her mother stopped herself and gave Linnie a strange look, not quite a smile. She turned back to the ledger on the table. "Never mind, now," she said. "Go be nice to Darla for a while."

Slowly, Linnie went upstairs. Darla was cross-legged on the bed, hugging Flat Mabel. When Linnie came in she began to inspect the doll seam by seam, as if she were interested in how it was made.

"What's the matter?" Linnie said.

"Nothing."

"Mom said you were going home."

"I am not." Darla turned around and looked out the window. "I'm going to Indiana."

"That's what I said." Linnie ran her fingers along the stack of books near the corner of her dresser. *Linnie's library,* her mother had said. Was there really a window seat? She sat down on the end of the bed by Darla. "Did your folks buy a house or get an apartment or what?"

"We're going to live out in the country," Darla said, making a fist and poking the mattress. "On a farm, sort of. With chickens."

Linnie wrinkled her forehead. "I didn't know your father was a farmer," she said. "I thought he had a job in Indianapolis."

"He does. He'll go to work every day and there I'll be with my mother and two acres of chickens. Yesterday I got this letter that said they had looked at three good places to rent, and one of them was out in the country. So I prayed that wouldn't be the one, but it was. And just look where you're going to get to live, and you don't even appreciate it. It isn't fair!" She poked the mattress again, and flung Flat Mabel aside so that she could lie down.

Linnie frowned, in sympathy for Flat Mabel. "Chickens are nice," she said.

"They are not," Darla said, raising her voice. "They smell. They give me creepy feelings, just the way dogs do. You never know when they might turn on you and attack."

"Are you *afraid* of chickens?" Linnie asked.

Darla was silent, with her face in the bedspread.

"Are you afraid of dogs?" Linnie pressed.

Darla turned over. "In Pittsburgh," she said, "I always carried my baton to school. Just in case there were dogs along the way."

Linnie smiled. Giggles came crowding into her throat in

place of the sour misery that had been there most of the day. She had a sudden vision of Darla the brave twirling along to school, on the lookout for vicious beagles and leaping dachshunds. She let herself bounce down onto the bed, laughing.

"You really were afraid of the puppies, weren't you? All along. That's why you kicked at Bess that time, and why you didn't help me look for Harry tonight and why you've never wanted to pet him or anything. You were too scared to touch him, even. And you told *me* to grow up!"

Darla sat up and tossed her head. "I'm not really afraid," she said. "I'm just cautious. And I would, too, touch Harry."

Linnie stopped laughing. "You'd have to find him first," she said. All her unhappiness came back to her. She lay flat and began to stare at the familiar cracks in the ceiling. "Arnold and I are going to look for him again in the morning," she said.

Darla got up and found her toothbrush. "I'll help you," she said. "I promise."

"Sure," mumbled Linnie, without really hearing Darla. She was busy listening inside herself for the whimper of a lost dog and wondering if she could bear never to see Harry again.

Unhappy Birthday

I'm ten. The thought fluttered in Linnie's mind while she was only half awake. Ten seemed so much older than nine. Advanced. She wiggled her fingers and toes to see if her body had noticed the change. Nothing. She waited a moment more, hoping for the special birthday feeling that she remembered from other years, an awareness that the day was hers alone and everyone knew it, a tingly sensation of importance.

Darla stirred beside her, and Linnie's eyes snapped open. Yesterday came back into her mind a bit at a time—the house, Harry, everything. No wonder the birthday feeling wouldn't come. The sun wasn't even shining. She slipped out of bed and began to get dressed, with one eye to the window. The sky was dull and gray, with a darker rim. It couldn't rain today, she thought; it wouldn't dare. It wouldn't dare *storm*, would it? The clouds made her hurry, and she didn't take time to wake Darla.

Aunt Em let her have cake and orangeade for breakfast. That meant "happy birthday," Linnie knew, even though Aunt Em didn't say it.

Linnie tried not to think about how it would be to eat

breakfast at the house in Springtown, with no Aunt Em to fix it.

"Your mom and dad went to town already," Aunt Em said, pouring herself a cup of tea. "They wanted me to tell you they'd bring home some ice cream tonight, and that you've got a package or two coming. Or three, if they get their last-minute shopping done." She eased down into the kitchen rocker, balancing her cup. "And your granpop," she said, "he's gone up to Fiddler's to ask around about that dog."

"Oh, good." Linnie ate faster and felt better, thinking about Granpop and the men who came to the garage with their tractors and ailing trucks and noisy cars. Maybe one of them had found Harry, or had seen him, at least. The idea gave her fresh energy.

"I've got to go see Arnold Anderson," she said, with her mouth full.

"Not likely," Aunt Em said. "It's getting set to rain."

"No, it's not," argued Linnie. "Not yet. Anyway, I'll wear my sweater."

Aunt Em frowned. "Might be a storm," she said. "You'd better stay in."

The back of Linnie's neck began to prickle. She thought about little Harry, shaking with each roll of thunder. "It won't storm," she said. She got up and grabbed her sweater off its hook behind the door, and left without giving Aunt Em any more time for warnings. "I'll be careful," she called back over her shoulder.

The last she heard was Aunt Em at the door, hollering. "If it starts to storm, you get in somewhere! You hear me, child? Get in and stay there!"

Linnie went the long way around to Arnold's house,

whistling for Harry and listening for thunder. The leaves were nervous, turning up their light undersides, but the clouds were quiet. Thank goodness for that, Linnie thought as she knocked on the Andersons' door. But then she had to wait for Arnold's mother to wake him up; he had come back from doing his papers and flopped back into bed.

Linnie sat on the top step of the Andersons' porch and worried about things. For a while she practiced feeling lonely, which was how she was going to be when she lived in Springtown without Arnold and without a dog. She had just switched to making up sad poems in her head when a familiar green truck spluttered by and crunched into the gravel parking area beside the store.

"Arnold!" called Linnie through the screen. "I'll be right back!"

She ran. Maybe Harry was found. She hoped he was, so that she could see him; and she hoped he wasn't, so that he wouldn't have to be in a cage, waiting for whatever might happen to him. It was such an effort of hoping that her heart thumped, and thumped even harder when she tried to stretch herself up to see into the window at the back of the truck.

"What's the trouble here?" The dogcatcher's voice was so close to her ear that Linnie jumped again, without meaning to. He had a bottle of cream soda and a bag of cheese crackers which he put into the front seat of the truck. "Just gettin' my breakfast," he said.

"Oh," she said. "Uh–hi, Mr. Sparks. I was just wondering if you found that puppy you were looking for last week. The one my Aunt Em called you about."

"See for yourself," he said, and hoisted her up. There

was only one dog in his collection, and it was big and white and sick-looking.

"Aw," she said. "Poor thing." But she almost floated back down to ground level. Harry wasn't there. He was free, at least. If only he could be safe, too.

"Might be I'll still find him today," Mr. Sparks said. "I'm on my way over toward Two Forks to pick up a little dog that got hit by a car last night. Doesn't seem to be hurt too much, though. That's what the fella said when he called."

The liveliness in Linnie's chest grew still. "What color was it?"

"Don't rightly remember. Brown, maybe."

She nodded and tried to blink the sudden sting out of her eyes.

"Might be the one, might not," he said. "That first one you saw in the truck last week, now, that one's happy as a clam. Mrs. Teddricks liked her right off. Named her Queenie, fixed her a fancy bed, and everything." He squinted down at Linnie and hesitated. "What you cryin' for?" he asked.

Linnie hiccuped. "It's my birthday," she said. "I'm ten."

Morrison Sparks wrinkled his forehead until his brows met in a V of puzzlement. "Many happy returns," he said, ". . . I guess." He stepped up into his truck and drove away, with gravel spinning out behind the tires.

"Hey, Linnie!" Arnold came up on his bicycle just as the truck went out of sight. "Did Sparks get him yet?"

"Not yet."

"Well," said Arnold, before she could go on, "we'd better put off our search for a while, is what I think. There's an honest-to-grapefruit whopper of a storm coming. You better go home, right now. My mother had the radio on and there was this awful static, like you couldn't hear a thing, and then some sort of special announcement except you couldn't hear that, either, and—listen to that!"

The sky grumbled in the voice of a faraway lion, hungry. A meat-eater. Linnie felt her knees loosen, so that she wobbled where she stood, under an umbrella of clouds that had changed their tint and grown unruly without her notice.

"Hop on," Arnold said, patting the package carrier on the rear fender of his bike. "I'll give you a ride."

Linnie didn't hesitate. There was a rule at her house that said no riding double, but that didn't bother her now. "I'm on," she said, and they went swaying around the corner and down the street toward Granpop's with Arnold standing up to pedal and Linnie holding her feet out on either side.

At the corner of the orchard they met Darla, running. She waved them to a stop with a proud-as-Miss-America smile. "I did it," she said. "Come see."

Linnie slid off Arnold's bike. "Did what?" she said, with an anxious upward look.

"Come see," Darla repeated.

Arnold wheeled around in the middle of the road while thunder announced the first sprinkles of rain. "Tell me later," he said and pumped hard for home. In the west a crooked line of white flashed earthward.

"We have to get in," Linnie said, shivering, trying to make her voice behave.

"Come on, you scaredy-cat. It's barely even raining yet." Darla tweaked at her sleeve. "You'll hate yourself if you don't see this. I mean it."

"Where?" Linnie wanted to shut her eyes and plug her ears and be safe and dry, but Darla kept pulling so that she had to run with her.

"In the garage!" Darla called.

"Girls!" came Aunt Em's frantic voice. "Girls! Come in!"

"This way!" urged Darla, tugging Linnie into Jack Tramp's lane and then, finally, to shelter.

Linnie gulped for breath and blinked in the dim light. With the sky so dark outside, it was almost night in the garage. It took her a moment to notice a small shadow moving on the floor, whining, snuffling at her feet. Harry.

"See? I found him!" Darla crowed. "He was just nosing around in the weeds on the other side of the road. Just right there, like he was waiting or something."

For a moment, the threat of the storm seemed to fade. The pup was all Linnie could see, all she could hear. She went down on her knees and gathered him into her arms. He flattened himself against her and trembled.

"It's all right, Harry," she whispered. "Everything's okay, Harry. You're safe with me now."

"There," said Darla, "you've seen him. Come on now. Let's get back to the house before it really starts to rain."

New thunder roared above the garage; a loose window rattled. Linnie tightened her arms around the dog to keep herself from shaking so. "We can't go out in a storm like this," she said. "That would be dumb. We'll just stay here until it's over." The window rattled again, and Linnie held her breath until it stopped. Harry pressed his nose against the inside of her arm.

"Uck!" Darla complained. "You mean you want to stay in this little rickety place? It'll probably fall right down on top of us. Anyway, it smells." She pushed the door open and held out her hand, palm up. "Come on, Linnie. It isn't even raining hard yet." She took one step outside. "It isn't that far. Run!"

Linnie shook her sweater off her shoulders and wrapped it around Harry. "Darla," she said, getting up and moving to the door, "don't–"

But Darla was already running, and Linnie didn't have time to decide. *Stay there,* said Aunt Em's voice, silent but clear, in her mind.

"Hurry!" yelled Darla.

Linnie took a step outside. The raindrops were still light and bouncy. Not bad. She gathered up her courage and clutched Harry in his bundle and ran after Darla.

And suddenly, from nowhere and everywhere at once, the wind slammed down.

The Flash and the Roar

Linnie lost her balance and fell at the edge of the lane; she could feel the gravel cutting through the knees of her jeans. She screamed but the sound blew away, drowned in a swirl of water. Her glasses got wet as a windshield, so that everything blurred. She fumbled for a better grip on her sweater with the dog inside, found her feet, and turned back to the corner of Jack Tramp's abandoned house, pressing herself against it in the hope that it would keep her from being tumbled across the road like one more loose twig.

From the corner of her eye she saw a flash of color—Darla's red slacks—that ran and stopped and ran again toward the front porch at home. Granpop's maple trees swayed like dancers in a chorus line. They bent over the running blotch of red, snapped up, bent again. The darting figure hesitated once more.

"Darla, hurry!" screamed Linnie.

And then the tree by the driveway swayed too far. Its trunk split in a great jagged crack. The top shuddered and fell into the yard. A jungle of tossing green branches lay between Linnie and the safety of Granpop's house. And somewhere beneath it was Darla.

Lightning sizzled overhead, and thunder exploded, very near. Linnie forgot to breathe. People really did die of fright, didn't they? Her arms and legs refused to move. The only spot of life about her was the warmth against her stomach, where Harry had come unwrapped. For his sake, she licked her lips. "It's all right, Harry," she said. "Don't shake so."

The wind passed as quickly as it had come, but the rain came harder. It poured over Linnie, straight down, heavy, and grew to a waterfall from the edge of the roof. What she wanted was to get inside. Get in, get dry. Be safe. But—oh, Darla! Another dazzle of lightning, another thunderclap. Linnie had never fainted in her whole life, but she thought this was the time.

The little dog's toenails scrabbled through her shirt to the skin. "What'll we do, Harry?" she whispered. "What'll we do?" Her fingers loosened enough to rub his head, which was getting wet even under the sweater.

Over the sound of the rain came a cry, forlorn as a fallen bird. "Help! Lin-niee! Help!"

Think, Linnie said to herself. Think. Her breath came hard. She could get herself back to Jack Tramp's garage, she was sure, and save herself. Or she might circle out around the fallen tree and make a run for Granpop's back door. *Crack!* went the lightning.

"Help me! Linnie?—Linnie?"

Linnie swallowed and felt sick. What if Darla's bones were broken? she thought. What if there was blood? Panic fell on her, heavy as the rain. Thunder rolled again, and Linnie saw someone on the porch, wading down into the green maple sea, shoving, pulling. But it was too much for Aunt Em. The tree didn't move, and Darla didn't come up out of it. Maybe if I could pull, too . . . , Linnie thought, and then she thought again. It was a big tree. Even together, she and Aunt Em wouldn't be able to handle it.

Linnie hugged Harry and tried to ignore the numbness of her feet and the cold wetness of her arms. She knew what she ought to do. She ought to step away from the little bit of shelter she had found and run through the storm, up the road to Fiddler's Garage. Granpop must be there still; if he had been home, he would have come out to help Aunt Em. Surely someone would be at Fiddler's, anyway, someone who could help.

"Oh, Harry," she said, "I can't do it. I can't possibly do it." Thunder echoed from two directions at once, hemming her in. He whimpered, and she began to stroke him, arranging the sweater so that he had more room to breathe.

"Poor little thing," she said, and somehow her feet began to move, taking her away from the side of Jack Tramp's house. One step, another step, three. If she looked up, she thought, that would be the end of it. But if she concentrated on Harry—"It's all right, boy. It's okay. It's not far"—then maybe she could make it. He really did need her. He was the one that would die of fright, without her.

She began to run through the pounding rain, stumbling, making her way around fallen branches, clutching Harry and talking to him nonstop. "In a minute, Harry. Almost there, now. Don't be afraid. I'm here."

Fiddler's Garage seemed farther away than it had ever been, almost as if it were something in a dream, floating always just out of reach. Her head began to hurt, and her chest tightened, so that she had to whisper to Harry. Then, finally, she could see the wide doors standing open, with a cluster of men watching the storm from inside.

"Granpop!" gasped Linnie, and splashed across a puddle to throw herself against him, dripping like an unsqueezed sponge. The dog wriggled free of her sweater and tried to hide under her arm.

"What the—?" Granpop held her at arm's length.

"Tree down," she panted. "Help—Darla—in front—yard." Each breath stabbed her side. "Aunt—Em—can't move it." Before the words were out, she heard the grinding start of Fiddler's tow truck. Three men crowded into the cab, and Granpop hopped onto the running board.

"Stay here!" he shouted to her. "Stay in out of this!" It was the fastest that Linnie had ever seen him move.

Suddenly the truck was gone, zigzagging down the littered street and past the orchard. Then her legs wouldn't hold her, and she sat down right where she was, between the air hose and the grease rack.

"Harry," she whispered, "oh, Harry," and held him close to keep away the thunder.

Many Happy Returns

By noon the sun was shining and Darla was complaining that she couldn't twirl her baton at all with so many Band-Aids on her hands. Aunt Em lost patience and snapped that Darla was lucky to have hands at all.

"Imagine," she said for what seemed like the hundredth time, "a whole tree falls on her and she doesn't have anything but a few little cuts and scratches. Not one of the big limbs touched her."

"I'm bruised," Darla reminded them. "It was the little limbs that did it. I'm bruised all over. It just doesn't show yet. I was pinned under there for *ages.*"

Most of the maple top was still filling the front yard, giving everything a look of strange disorder. Some of the gutter had been knocked off the edge of the roof and hung at odd angles. Two sides of the house were polka-dotted with bits of leaves, and the garden had turned into a pond.

In spite of everything, Linnie thought, her birthday was turning out better than she had expected. Dad and Mom and Garrett had come home to check on the damage and exclaim over Darla's escape.

"Boy, is she lucky," Garrett said to anyone who would listen. "That tree just missed the wires. You're all lucky. If there had been live wires tangled in that wet tree—wow, look out!"

Linnie worked at drying Harry with an old towel that Aunt Em had said she could use, which was a miracle in itself because sooner or later Aunt Em would have to wash that towel, dog germs and all. Then there was lunch, cold because the power was out. Mom said if Linnie would put the dog in the woodshed and come to the table, she could open her birthday presents.

Darla kept talking about how it felt to be caught under a fallen treetop, with all the branches poking at you. "I didn't even see it coming," she said. "Do you know what a shock that was?"

Linnie didn't say that she had seen it. Whenever she blinked, the image of the falling tree was still there as if it were printed on the underside of her eyelids. She stopped listening to Darla, who was repeating herself a lot, and started on the three boxes that Mom had brought.

Two books in the first one, a new polka-dot blouse in the second. She opened the third package and frowned. "What's this?" she said, rummaging in the tissue paper. "A belt?"

"Keep going," her dad said. Suddenly everyone was watching her.

She pulled out the belt and it wasn't a belt at all. It was a leash, with a dog collar clipped to the end.

"It was supposed to be an IOU present," Mom said. "Like a promise. I mean, we'd been considering having a dog in the new house, anyway. After all, the backyard's fenced in. And then yesterday, when we saw how important it was to you—"

Linnie's mouth hung open. "You mean—?" she whispered. "All along, you were thinking maybe—?" But the rest of the words wouldn't come.

Dad nodded. "It seems to me, though," he said, "and your granpop agrees with me, that you've got your dog picked out already. It's a long time before we'll be moving, but I suppose if you wanted to be extra careful with him until—"

Linnie interrupted with a squeal. "You mean I can keep Harry? I really can? Aunt Em, can I? Oh, that would be the best thing!"

"Don't you dare to bring him in this house again," Aunt Em said. "I'll skin him. I'll skin you both." She didn't smile, but it wasn't the same as *no*.

"You'll have to use the woodshed, Linnie," her mother said, "and break him to papers or something, or he can't be in the new house, either."

"He's a nice little dog," Granpop said. "Lot of terrier in him, I judge. Some beagle, too. I expect he'll be a lot of trouble when it storms, though."

"Oh, I'll take extra care of him then," Linnie promised. "I won't let him howl or anything."

Garrett got up and stretched. "Where did you put this mutt?" he asked. "If he's joining the family, I guess I want a better look at him than I got yesterday."

Darla examined her Band-Aids, looking cross. "Just remember who found him this morning," she said.

All the way to the bus station with Mom and Aunt Em

and Darla, Linnie rehearsed what she would say. *Good-by, Darla. I'm sorry you got hurt while you were here. It was nice having you.* Maybe she should cross her fingers for that part. No. Maybe she should say, *It was an interesting visit, Darla.* That was close to the truth, at least. *Come back again, Darla.* That would be the polite thing, but she didn't think Darla would want to. Thank goodness.

Aunt Em stayed in the car while Mom went to see the ticket agent about Darla's fare. "You have a safe trip, now," Aunt Em said, "and remember me to your mother and dad."

Darla was all sweet and fluttery, waving butterfly fingers at Aunt Em, being the main character in a movie-screen farewell.

"I'll miss you," she called over her shoulder. "I hate to go."

How soppy, Linnie thought. All that Darla hated was the idea of living with chickens. If I were Darla, Linnie started to think, and then stopped herself. If she were Darla, she guessed she wouldn't be very happy, either. After all, she knew something about how it felt to be moving.

"Here," she said, reaching for Darla's suitcase. "Let me help." The bus stood at the curb, waiting. "Good-by," Linnie said, keeping her eyes down. "I guess I never did say thanks for finding Harry and all that. But you know how much I—well—and I know that you didn't even like to get close to him or anything, and—"

"Linnie." Darla dropped the tilt of her chin. "I really have to tell you about that," she said. "I know I let you think that I picked him up and carried him over to the garage that morning, but I—I just couldn't."

Linnie raised her eyes. "How, then?"

"Promise you won't tell Arnold?"

"Why not?"

"I wouldn't want to hurt his feelings. It was so nice of him to give me chocolate and everything."

Linnie put one hand over her mouth.

"What I did," Darla said, "was, after I saw the dog, I ran back upstairs and got that bag of candy and broke off little pieces of it and laid it down like a trail right up to the garage door. And Harry followed along and ate every bit. He's a pig, Linnie. I hope your folks can afford to feed him. And don't tell Arnold, but that candy had a very peculiar odor. I couldn't possibly have eaten any of it myself."

Linnie was still pretending to cough when Mom came running with Darla's ticket. There was another little flurry of good-bys and messages for Darla's parents. Then it was time, and Darla was on the bus, waving from a middle window, mouthing some words that Linnie couldn't understand. And then, at last, she was gone.

"Are you sure you have to move?" asked Arnold. He was stretched out flat in Granpop's backyard while Harry, tethered to the clothesline, trotted around and over him, stopping for a scratch right in the middle of Arnold's T-shirt.

Linnie picked a dandelion and tickled Harry's nose. "Not till fall," she said. "Fall" had a comfortable, faraway sound to it. "That's a long time yet."

"Yeah," said Arnold and squinched up his face to save his eyes from puppy feet. "I'll sure miss this old thunder-pup, though."

"You'll see him," Linnie promised. "We'll be here a lot, Arnold. It's not as if we were going clear to Indianapolis or something. It's more like having two homes instead of one. That's what Granpop says, anyway."

"Yeah," said Arnold again. "I guess it would be. Two houses and a dog. Some people have all the luck."

"Me?" Linnie pushed her glasses back where they belonged. "Lucky?"

"You can even spell," he said. "It's not fair." Arnold tried to get his sleeve out of Harry's mouth. "You know what Darla told me yesterday when everyone else was busy cleaning up the tree? She said she almost wished her arm had got broken or something, so she would have to stay longer."

"You're making that up," Linnie said.

"Am not. She's the one that said you were lucky. At first she thought you were spoiled, but then she decided it was just lucky. She didn't even want to come here at first, she said, but her parents made her and then she got to liking it. She said she thought for sure she was going to die under that tree because you'd be too scared to do anything. She couldn't get over it, how you went up to Fiddler's right in the middle of the storm and everything."

"Arnold!" Linnie gave him a fierce look. "Did Darla really say all that?"

He grinned. "Most of it."

"I'll bet." Maybe, though, thought Linnie, just maybe, she ought to write to Darla, and then Darla might write back to her, and who could tell how it might turn out? Harry quit chewing on Arnold and climbed into Linnie's lap, where he tied himself in a soft knot, nose to tail, and closed his eyes.

Linnie heard the back screen sighing open and banging shut, the way it always did. Heels thumped on the concrete walk that came to the end of the clothesline.

"Arnold Anderson," Aunt Em said, "your mother just called and said for you to get yourself home."

"Do I have to?"

"Right this minute, she said."

"Aw, bananas!" Arnold rolled to his feet, claimed his bicycle from its parking spot by the lilac bush, and began to ride in and out and around the clothesline poles, ducking the wire as he went.

"Quit that!" Aunt Em called. "It makes tracks in the grass. Go on! Go home!"

The clatter and the calling woke Harry, who tumbled over Linnie's knee and trotted off as far as his rope would reach.

"Hmp!" said Aunt Em. "Not you, you fool dog. You belong here, I guess."

Linnie smiled. She was lucky, all right. She felt like shouting and singing and bouncing around. She almost felt like turning a cartwheel. But she settled for a whistle and a snap of her fingers, and Harry came running, ready for anything.